THE
FORBIDDEN
DUKE

❧ *The Untouchables* ❧

DARCY
BURKE

Copyright

The Forbidden Duke
Copyright © 2016 Darcy Burke
All rights reserved.
ISBN: 1944576010
ISBN-13: 9781944576011

Book design © Darcy Burke.
Cover design © Carrie Divine/Seductive Designs.
Photo copyright: Couple © Novelstock.com
Photo copyright: Stairs © Stanislav Bokach/Depositphotos.com
Editing: Linda Ingmanson.

For Mr. Wright
Thank you for making middle school
survivable
and for making the study of history
such an important part of my life.

Chapter One

St. Ives, England, February, 1811

MISS ELEANOR LOCKHART stared at her father in open shock. "You have nothing left?"

Davis Lockhart pulled at his sleeve, a familiar gesture that practically screamed his discomfort with this interview. "Not *nothing*, but not enough to support this household." He turned apologetic, murky brown eyes on her. "And not enough to support you."

Nora stared at him from the recesses of the ancient settee, whose broken leg was propped up with a stack of books. He'd lost all his money—or almost all, apparently—to a bad investment scheme. "What was it again?" she asked, shaking her head.

Father had always been a bit of a scatterbrain, but she hadn't realized the depth of his ineptitude when it came to financial matters.

He coughed. "A building situation in Sussex."

That sounded terribly vague. Unfortunately, she suspected he couldn't provide a more detailed description, likely because he didn't know one.

"What am I to do, then?" She asked the question plainly, without emotion, despite the thundering of her heart and the fear spreading through her limbs as she contemplated what her future might be. With no husband and nothing but a scandal-laden past to her credit, Nora had few options.

Father straightened and turned toward the window overlooking their small property on the edge of town. He leased the cottage and its surrounding garden. It was home—where Nora and her sister had grown up, where they'd plotted their exciting futures as countesses or duchesses, where Nora had returned, defeated, after leaving London in ruin in the midst of her second Season. It was where Nora had presumed she would live her spinster life, until such time as she had to find her own smaller cottage with the modest income her father left her. However, that was not to be.

"Your sister would surely take you in," Father said without looking at her.

Nora doubted it, not because Joanna wouldn't want to, but because her husband, the vicar, would likely disallow it. Nora was a pariah, a loose woman who'd been caught kissing a gentleman who wasn't her husband or her fiancé. She was not the sort of woman Matthias Shaw would invite to live in his vicarage.

"I find that unlikely," Nora said softly, her mind working even as her spirit was failing.

"Perhaps Cousin Frederick's wife will take you in."

Cousin Frederick who had died five years ago? He and his wife, the daughter of a baron, had sponsored Nora ten years earlier. They'd been kind and generous, and Nora had dreadfully and mortifyingly humiliated them with her scandalous behavior. They'd shipped Nora back to St. Ives immediately following her fall from grace with the explicit instructions that they would *not* be sponsoring Jo.

Since Cousin Frederick's death, his wife Clara had remarried, and Nora couldn't imagine she would reopen her home to the woman whose behavior had utterly embarrassed her. Perhaps when the gates to the Underworld were coated in frost.

Nora didn't even bother responding to her father's ridiculous suggestion. Instead, she tossed him a glower and gritted her teeth behind tightly closed lips.

He smiled in return. Rather it was a pained stretching of his mouth which only underscored how much he disliked confrontation, especially with his daughters. "I suppose you could find a position as a lady's companion or perhaps a governess."

He made the comment blithely, as if such employment grew on trees and were ripe for the picking. "Just how am I to do that?"

His brow pleated, and his eyes darkened. "How am I to know? You'll work it all out. You're a smart gel, like your mother was." His tone softened. He wasn't a particularly sentimental father, but Nora knew he'd loved her mother and still missed her, though it had been twenty years since her death.

Nora stood, intending to go and speak with her sister at once. Jo might not have any suggestions, but she at least possessed a sympathetic ear. The only one Nora had.

The afternoon was cool and overcast, but Nora was quite warm from her walk by the time she reached the vicarage on the other side of the village. Jo's housekeeper, Mrs. Kettler, showed Nora to the small sitting room to await her sister.

A moment later, Jo entered, her dark brown hair swept into a neat style, her hazel eyes sharp and assessing. "I wasn't expecting you today."

What she didn't say was that her husband didn't like surprises, particularly from Jo's outcast sister. "I know. I needed to speak with you urgently. We can go for a walk if you'd prefer."

Jo's brows dipped. "What's the matter?"

Nora saw no need to prevaricate. Jo knew their father's flaws as well as anyone. "Father has lost his money in an investment scheme. He is moving to a small cottage on his brother-in-law's farm in Dorset."

Jo's eyes flashed surprise. "Indeed? I didn't think Aunt Polly cared for Father."

Polly was Father's younger sister, and they did not get on well. Nora and Jo had met her all of four times in their entire lives. "He's going to live in a tiny cottage on the far reaches of their sheep pasture. I daresay she will avoid him as much as possible."

"Still, it's kind of her to take him in," Jo said.

That was true. And while the cottage they were allowing Father to live in wasn't large enough to accommodate Nora, perhaps they had room in their house. Furthermore, they had children. Perhaps they needed a governess. Nora nearly laughed at that thought. They weren't the sort to have a governess. They lived in the country because they preferred a simple life.

Jo gestured for Nora to leave the sitting room with her. "Let's take that walk." She went into the entryway, where she donned gloves and a hat. "Will I be warm enough?"

Nora was wearing one of the few serviceable gowns she owned—a light wool—and nothing else for added warmth. "You'll be chilly at first, but you'll warm up."

Jo nodded and opened the door for Nora to precede her outside. "Are you going with him to Dorset?"

The sun was now peeking through the clouds. Nora tipped her head down so that the rim of her bonnet shaded her eyes. "There isn't room for me. I have to find another arrangement."

Jo stopped in her tracks, turning to stare at Nora. "You can't mean—"

Nora touched her younger sister's arm gently. "No, I do not expect to live with you. I know Matthias would never allow it."

Jo exhaled, her expression pained. "I'm sorry."

"Don't be. It's my fault you're married to such a stiff-neck anyway." Because Nora's ruinous behavior had ruined her chances for a Season.

Jo frowned as she glanced back toward the vicarage. "Don't say that. I know you see him as unforgiving and judgmental, which I agree are not the best traits for a vicar," she said wryly. "However, he's a kind husband. I could do far worse."

I could be unmarried like you.

The unspoken words invaded Nora's brain and took up residence. This was not the life she'd planned. Alone. Lonely. And now with an absolutely unknown future before her. All because she'd flirted with the wrong man and foolishly accepted his love-soaked, specious invitation to meet him privately. She'd quite made her own mess.

Nora started walking again, and they made their way along the narrow lane that led to the vicarage before cutting across the field to a shallow stream where they liked to take picnics in the summer. "Anyway, I was hoping you could help me think of something. I doubt Aunt Polly would take me in."

Jo made a face. "You wouldn't want to live on a sheep farm. I don't suppose Cousin Clara would allow you to live with her, not after what happened. No, that way is closed I think."

Firmly. Nora nodded in agreement. "Father suggested I become a governess or a lady's companion."

"That's not a terrible notion," Jo said. "Is experience required for such work?"

Nora shrugged. "How difficult could it be? Especially as a lady's companion?"

Jo winced. "Will your...past be an issue in obtaining this sort of employment?"

Nora exhaled. "I don't know. But I don't seem to have any other choice. I shall write to an agency in London and make an inquiry."

"Perhaps you should use a different name—maybe take Mother's."

Nora smiled as she cast a sidelong glance toward her sister. "And become Eleanor Godbehere?" They giggled together.

Jo shook her head. "Poor Mother had the most tragic surname."

And ill-fitting since God hadn't seemed to be anywhere around when she'd succumbed to a long and particularly painful illness when Nora had been just seven and Jo only five.

As they neared the stream, Nora stopped and stared at her younger sister, whose life she'd also inadvertently ruined nine years ago. "I think I'd prefer to be honest about who I am. Disingenuousness is what led me into disaster in the first place." She'd told Cousin Clara, her sponsor, that she was going to the retiring room with another young lady. Instead, Nora had gone to the library to meet Lord Haywood, the man she'd fancied herself in love with.

Jo strolled to the edge of the water. "I suppose that's the best thing to do." She smiled at Nora. "You are not at all the foolish girl you were nine years ago."

"Thank goodness, no." Nora shuddered to think of that wide-eyed, naïve young lady. If she could go back and behave differently, she'd do it in a trice. She bent and picked up a smooth rock, then joined Jo where she skipped the stone into the brook with a flick of her wrist.

"Will you be at all anxious to be in London?" Jo asked.

Nora thought about what she might say or do if she saw the people who'd been so quick to disdain her, or worse, if she encountered Lord Haywood. She shook her head. She was getting ahead of herself. "I may not even end up working in London."

"If you're to be a companion, I daresay that's precisely where you'll be, especially with the Season starting."

Yes, that would be the best arrangement. The thought of returning to London—the dinner parties, the promenades, the balls— was a bit daunting, but it would also be a change of pace from the lonely life she'd inhabited in St. Ives. It was also far better than a sheep pasture.

"You'll write to me every day?" Jo asked, her gaze earnest and intense. "I will write to you too—for support."

Nora nudged Jo's arm as they stood side by side facing the stream. She was immeasurably glad to have this one ally. "I will."

"I wish Mother hadn't died," Jo said quietly, her gaze directed at the water, her mouth turned down at the corners.

Nora put her arm around Jo's shoulders. "I wish that too, but at least we have each other."

Jo turned a warm smile toward her sister. "We do, and we always will. Even if you aren't anxious about London, I am. I don't want to see you hurt again."

Nora appreciated Jo's concern more than she could know. She let go of Jo and squatted down to pick up another rock. "It's unlikely anything like that would happen again—I've quite learned my lesson." She tossed the rock into the stream.

Jo clapped her hand over her mouth. When she dropped it, she said, "You shouldn't tempt fate like that."

No, she shouldn't, but it seemed Nora didn't know any other way.

❧❦❧

TITUS ST. JOHN, fifth Duke of Kendal, sat
alone in his private dining chamber at
Brooks's, the way he always did when he
had to be in town. It was one of the few
public activities he allowed himself, not that
it was remotely public. Muted harmonies of
laughter and conversation drifted to his
ears whenever a footman opened the door
to bring him his meal or replenish his
whisky. He didn't find the sounds inviting.
No, he found them largely grating, which
some, who had known him in his youth,
would find odd. He'd once been drawn to
such conviviality like a bird to a bright,
fragrant flower.

As a young buck and the Marquess of
Ravenglass before his father's death, he'd
taken advantage of everything his title and
wealth could offer. He'd gambled. He'd
spent exorbitant sums. He'd developed a
ghastly reputation as a rake. He'd enjoyed
himself immensely until a series of events
had knocked him completely and
irrevocably off his self-constructed
pedestal. Since then, he'd turned his back
on all the things that had once defined him.

"Your Grace?"

Titus looked up at the footman who'd
entered and saw his stepfather moving over

the threshold beside him. "Good evening, Satterfield."

"Evening, Kendal." The earl nodded, his nearly bald head shining in the lamplight. "Your mother sends her best."

His stepmother, but really the only mother he'd ever known. Titus had been just five when she'd married his father, and she'd cared for Titus as if he'd been her own. She'd wed Satterfield nearly seven years ago, after a more than suitable two-year mourning period following Titus's father's death.

The footman poured a glass of whisky and handed it to Satterfield, then left.

Satterfield joined Titus near the fireplace, taking the chair opposite him. "Your mother also wanted me to harass you about coming to tea tomorrow, but I'm not going to do that."

Titus arched a brow at him over his whisky glass. "You just did."

"I *mentioned* it. This will save me great heartache with her as I can honestly say we discussed it. Wives are a complicated business." He gave Titus a meaningful glance that likely tried to communicate, *You'd know this if you were married.*

Titus's unwed state was the sole source of strife between him and his stepmother. Every time she wrote to him or saw him in person, she asked when he planned to take a wife. It was an obligatory conversation, one he was certain would take place tomorrow if he went to tea.

"Did she ask you to harass me about marriage too?"

Satterfield chuckled. "No. In fact, I think she's finally accepted your unmarried state. She's hiring a companion."

Titus leaned forward slightly. "Indeed? When did she decide this?"

"One of her friends suggested it recently—something, rather someone, to keep her occupied."

"Isn't that why she married you?" Titus asked drily. One of the things his stepmother always told him was that if he took a wife, he wouldn't be lonely anymore. Except Titus wasn't lonely; he was alone. They were not the same thing.

"There are certain activities I won't do, even under threat of torture, such as shopping." Satterfield shuddered. "Your mother adores shopping. Yes, she goes with friends, but a companion will be ever ready, you see."

Titus did see, and was quite pleased with this development. With a companion to manage, she would leave Titus alone when it came to marriage prospects. Splendid. He picked up his whisky. "Tell her I'll be at the tea."

The door opened swiftly and banged backward against the wall. A young chap, his cravat askew, stumbled inside. "This Fitzpatrick's room?" he slurred.

Titus took in the buck's disheveled hair and flushed cheeks and judged him thoroughly sotted. "No."

A second man, a few years older than the first, appeared behind the young man. He clasped the younger man's shoulder, his eyes narrowed and disapproving as he dragged him back over the threshold. "Christ, Lyndhurst, that's Kendal's room," he hissed. He glanced apologetically at Titus and muttered, "Sorry, Your Grace."

Titus nodded. "Do close the door behind you."

"Of course." The man, the Marquess of Axbridge, Titus believed, all but shoved the drunken Lyndhurst from the room, then closed the door as quietly as possible.

"Does their deference amuse you?" Satterfield asked, looking at him askance. He shook his head. "Bah, I know it doesn't."

No, it did not. It was, however, relieving, for it meant they cut him a wide berth. He had no patience for such ninnyhammer antics. When he'd shed his own dissolute behavior, he'd quite lost the ability to tolerate it from anyone else. And Society knew it.

"They're mostly harmless," Satterfield said.

"They are not, but I shan't debate it with you." Titus had seen firsthand the harm of such careless conduct, but he wouldn't disclose that to Satterfield. Not when he hadn't ever disclosed it to anyone. He finished his whisky and set the glass on a table next to his chair. "I believe I'm finished for tonight. Do stay as long as you like."

"Where are you headed?"

"Nowhere you'd care to accompany me." Titus was on his way to a soiree outside the realm of Polite Society where he would meet several courtesans. He typically spent his first weeks back in London searching for a mistress to keep for the Season. It could be a tedious endeavor, but necessary in order to find the right woman who would warm his bed without making demands, all while behaving in the most discreet manner possible. This was paramount to him. His business was no one's but his own.

"Just so," Satterfield said. "See you tomorrow, then."

Titus left the room, closing the door as he went into the now empty corridor. He made his way downstairs, and the men seated in the subscription room fell silent, save one who loudly whispered, "The Forbidden Duke?"

Titus didn't turn his head to see who'd uttered his nickname. He didn't turn his head to acknowledge anyone. He stared straight ahead and left the club, never wondering nor caring what anyone thought of him.

Chapter Two
❧•3•❧

A FORTNIGHT AFTER sending an inquiry to a London agency, Nora walked into the drawing room of Lady Satterfield's town house on Mount Street for her first interview as a lady's companion. She'd arrived via post chaise late yesterday.

Nora took in the magnificence of the drawing room with its tall windows cloaked with gold curtains overlooking the street, a myriad of landscape paintings that gave the space a welcome feeling of the outdoors, as well as gilt-edged mirrors that lent an expansive air to the already large chamber, and three ornate chandeliers, whose crystal sparkled and winked in the afternoon light.

It was as elegant as Cousin Frederick's had been, yet somehow more comfortable. Or maybe that was just Nora's maturity showing, that she wasn't intimidated by a fancy London house. She wasn't as green as she'd once been.

A moment later, Lady Satterfield entered the drawing room. She was tall, with dark hair and a regal bearing, but also a warm smile that lent her approachability. Nora immediately relaxed.

"Good day, Miss Lockhart. I'm so pleased you could meet with me today. Please, sit." Lady Satterfield gestured toward a settee, while she sank into an armed chair covered with blue silk.

Nora perched on the edge. "Thank you, my lady. It is my pleasure to make your acquaintance."

"My butler is bringing tea in a moment. Do you know how to pour?"

Nora nodded. "I do, my lady."

"Excellent. I thought as much, since you've been out in Society."

The countess made the statement without inflection, making it impossible for Nora to infer what her opinion might be of Nora's past. And she didn't think for a moment that the agency hadn't informed Lady Satterfield of Nora's indiscretions. Nora had been honest and forthright when she'd inquired with them, and they'd been just as direct in their response, telling her that placement might be difficult.

Yet, here she was with an interview.

She rushed to answer Lady Satterfield, even though she hadn't asked a direct question. "Yes, I was out in Society for two Seasons." Not quite, but close enough.

"The agency informed me of your past

experience."

Again, Nora couldn't tell what Lady Satterfield thought of any of it, but Lady Satterfield's invitation to today's appointment had to mean that she wasn't bothered. Still, she'd feel better to have the issue out in the open. "You're aware of the circumstances under which I left London?"

Lady Satterfield looked at her with…kindness? Yes, her eyes crinkled at the edges and her lips curved into a compassionate smile. "I am, and all I can say is that I'm sorry things worked out that way for you. We've all done foolish things in our youth, but most are fortunate to keep them private. Society is most unforgiving when it comes to women. Never mind that the man is at least equally accountable, or in some cases more so. It was Lord Haywood?"

An image of the exceedingly handsome Haywood, an Untouchable, rose in her mind. With his dazzling smile, blond, wavy hair, and golden tongue, he'd quite charmed her nine years ago. "Yes." She coughed softly to clear her suddenly cobwebbed throat. "I take full responsibility for my actions."

Lady Satterfield cocked her head to the side. "I admire your maturity. Did you hope to marry him?"

"Foolishly, yes." Nora didn't bother trying to hide the self-derision in her tone. "When he pledged his undying love and said he planned to make me his wife, I believed him. At the time, an assignation in the library with my future betrothed seemed a touch risky, but I thought my future was secure."

How wrong she'd been. They'd been caught in an embrace in that library—during a ball—and the occasion had been the *on dit* of the Season. Cousin Frederick had packed Nora back to the country two days later. Haywood, meanwhile, had only been obliged to leave town for the Season; his reputation had been salvageable. He'd even gone on to marry a few years later. Nora, on the other hand, had been utterly ruined. All over a kiss, and not a particularly good one at that.

Lady Satterfield shook her head and pursed her lips. "Men can be such clods."

Though simple, Lady Satterfield's statement stoked a long-dormant fire in Nora's soul. So few people cast any fault on the gentleman, preferring instead to lay all of the blame at Nora's feet. Was it possible she empathized with Nora's plight? "I've changed since then."

Obtaining acceptance, finding a husband, securing a place in Society—all that had seemed critically important. She had none of that, and yet she couldn't say she was completely unhappy. She had her garden, her books, and something most women didn't: relative freedom. Rather, she'd *had* those things.

The warmth returned to Lady Satterfield's gaze. "I can see that, dear. You comport yourself very well. I don't care what happened in the past. I only care what happens now. I am looking for a companion who will accompany me shopping, assist with correspondence and other secretarial-type matters, and provide companionship. Does this interest you?"

Nora had already formed a quick opinion of the countess—she liked her. How could she not when she was the first person to show Nora such compassion? Being this woman's companion would not be a hardship by any measure. "Yes, I should like that very much. I'm an excellent writer. My mother always praised my early handwriting. It's likely why I worked hard to improve my skill."

"How long ago did you lose your mother, dear?"

Nora's chest tightened very briefly. The pain had lessened over the years, but in some ways, that bothered Nora. She didn't miss her mother as much as she used to, and that felt wrong somehow. "It's been twenty years."

"I'm so sorry you lost her at such a young age. I had my own mother until just a few years ago." She smiled fleetingly. "I still miss her, but she had a lovely life."

The butler arrived with the tea then, setting the tray on a table between them. Nora asked how Lady Satterfield liked her tea, then set about preparing their cups accordingly.

"You are quite adept," Lady Satterfield said. "Tell me, why are you seeking employment?" She picked up her cup and sipped her tea.

Nora smoothed her skirt over her knees, even though the outmoded fabric was lying perfectly flat. She hated admitting the embarrassing truth, but again preferred to be candid. "My father is moving to Dorset at the end of the month and will no longer have space for me."

Lady Satterfield's lips pursed into a slight frown. "What a pity. I can't say that recommends him, in my opinion."

Nora appreciated the countess's support, but also couldn't help but feel like a charity case.

"And what have you been doing these past nine years?" Lady Satterfield asked.

"Reading, mostly. I also enjoy working in

the garden." She was going to miss that. She'd cultivated a healthy display of flowers and shrubbery. She was most proud of the roses.

"Have you been happy? That is, if not for the change in your circumstances, would you have continued on as you were?"

Nora had difficulty understanding why this woman was inquiring after her happiness. No one beyond Jo had ever cared. "I expect so. My sister hoped that I would marry eventually."

Lady Satterfield took another sip of her tea. "Is that what you wanted?"

Once, when she'd been a young lady, fresh in London, she'd nurtured dreams of marriage and children. But after her fall from grace, she'd lost all expectation of such a future, regardless of her sister's determination to have faith. "Originally, but I have no such aspirations now. I shall be quite content to serve as your lady's companion. That is, if you decide to hire me." Nora felt color rise in her cheeks. She didn't wish to be presumptuous.

"I most certainly do," Lady Satterfield said. "Can you move in immediately?"

Nora couldn't speak for a moment. "I'm…overwhelmed by your faith in me."

"You possess a lovely spirit as well as resilience and intelligence. I am not at all concerned you will repeat the mistakes of your past."

Joy and relief merged, and Nora couldn't contain her smile. "I shan't."

"Excellent. We shall need to move quickly since my ball is in just a few days, and you will need to attend, of course." Her gaze dropped to Nora's horribly outdated traveling costume. "I gather you'll need a new wardrobe?"

Nora winced. "I'm afraid I haven't needed fashionable clothing in recent years."

"That's quite all right, dear. I am rather inspired by this project—not to say you're a project, but I daresay you are."

Nora couldn't possibly be irritated with the woman's assessment, not when her gray eyes were sparkling with infectious enthusiasm. "It is my good fortune to be your project. Thank you ever so much for this opportunity."

"Excellent. After tea, we shall embark on our first shopping trip. I'll have Harley send for your things." Lady Satterfield shook her head, smiling. "But I'm getting ahead of myself. I'll show you upstairs to your room and give you a thorough tour of the house. We have an extensive library downstairs— you did say you like to read, didn't you?"

Everything was happening so fast, but

then that was good, wasn't it? Nora had
needed a new situation and quickly at that.
Now she had one.

She would be companion to a kind and
generous countess. She would have a new
wardrobe and access to a fabulous library.
So she would never be married or have a
family of her own.

That was fine, since she'd abandoned that
dream long ago.

❦

TITUS ARRIVED TEN minutes before his
stepmother's tea was due to begin. Harley,
the Satterfields' typically unflappable butler,
blinked, registering a moment's surprise at
seeing Titus.

"Your Grace, Lady Satterfield will be
delighted to see you. She is already in the
drawing room."

"Thank you, Harley. I'll see myself up."
Titus climbed the stairs to the first floor
and entered the drawing room, where his
stepmother was speaking with a maid.

When Lady Satterfield saw Titus, her eyes
lit, and her lips spread into a broad smile.
"Kendal, you came."

She came toward him, and Titus bussed
her cheek. "I told Satterfield I was coming.
Didn't he inform you?"

"He did, but I wasn't going to believe it until I saw you for myself." She looked up at him and brushed her hand across his shoulder. "You had a speck of lint."

"Thank you."

"No, thank *you*. I know events like my tea today are not of your particular interest."

He glanced around the drawing room, which the maid had just vacated. "Where is your companion?"

His stepmother had sent word that she'd hired someone. "She'll be down directly. You'll like her, I think."

Titus had no intention of getting to know the woman well at all, but supposed he must at least be polite for his stepmother's sake.

Lady Satterfield's gaze moved toward the door behind Titus. "Ah, here she is."

Titus turned. The companion was not at all what he expected. He'd anticipated a middle-aged woman with graying hair, perhaps wearing spectacles and a lace-edged cap. She at least ought to have been unremarkable, but this woman was the exact opposite. In fact, Titus might have expected to see her at the Cyprian ball he'd attended last night, if she'd been dressed quite differently. Instead, she wore a charming day dress that only hinted at the curves cloaked by the gentle drape of the fabric. But it was her eyes that captivated him, at once sharply inquisitive and lushly inviting. He would've spoken with her last night and perhaps even employed her.

However, this was neither a Cyprian ball, nor was he in the market for a mistress any longer.

His stepmother's voice drew him briskly and sharply back to the present. "Kendal, allow me to present my new companion, Miss Eleanor Lockhart."

As stunned as he'd been by the woman's appearance, he was aghast at her identity. He was also distinctly uncomfortable. Which he should be. She'd been utterly ruined by one of Titus's former inner circle, the idiot Haywood.

Led by Titus, their select group of bucks had gallivanted all over London, doing whatever they damn well chose. Titus had set the tone—gambling, racing, and romancing women had been among his chief pursuits. He'd thought nothing of flirting with and perhaps stealing a kiss or two from a young miss. It had been a foolish practice, as were most of their activities, and in retrospect, Titus was shocked he'd never been caught. But then he hadn't been as stupid as Haywood, whom Titus had encouraged in his endeavor to lead some poor young woman into an embrace. That poor young woman had been Miss Lockhart, and they'd been caught.

Haywood, coward that he was, hadn't risen to the occasion and offered for her. He'd needed a moneyed bride, and so he'd skulked off to the country to bide his time until he could try again. Three years later, he'd snagged a wealthy wife, while Miss Lockhart had been left with nothing, and worse—no chance for anything.

Masking his recognition and discomfiture, Titus offered a benign smile. "Good afternoon, Miss Lockhart. It's a pleasure to make your acquaintance." It was no lie—they'd never been formally introduced, despite his awareness of who she was.

Lady Satterfield pivoted to her young and distractingly attractive companion. "Nora, this is my stepson, His Grace, the Duke of Kendal."

Nora. A strong but feminine name. It suited her.

Miss Lockhart dipped a curtsey. "It is an honor to meet you, Your Grace."

Her behavior was completely appropriate—necessary even—but he didn't want her showing him deference. Which was silly since he expected that from everyone else. "The honor is mine."

She looked at him, her brown eyes the
color of his favorite tawny port, and he had
the sense no one had said such a thing to
her. And why should they when she'd been
a pariah? He wanted to ask what had
happened to her since that unfortunate
event. More importantly, he wanted to
know why she was here.

But he didn't.

At that moment, Harley announced the
first guests, and Lady Satterfield went to
greet them, taking Miss Lockhart with her.

Titus watched them go, then turned and
went to stand near the window closest to
the corner away from the entry point, away
from where people would congregate…just
away. He fixed his gaze on the street below
so that he could survey the arrivals. Why,
he wasn't sure. It wasn't as if he cared who
attended. Plus, his brain was completely
focused on Miss Lockhart and her present
circumstances.

The event that had caused her ruin may
not have been directly his fault, but he
should at least have inquired after her
welfare.

He stood near the window for a good
half hour. As usual, people cast glances in
his direction, but no one approached him.
Nor did he approach anyone else. His
stepmother would perhaps chastise him for

his aloofness, but only for a bit. She knew he preferred solitude, even if she didn't understand it.

Since his father had died and Titus had inherited the title, he'd thrown himself into his duty, as both a landowner and a member of the House of Lords. He enjoyed spending time with his steward on his estate and with his secretary when he was in London. Beyond that, he had no interest in friendships or relationships of any kind—save the mistress he took for the Season. He supposed it was odd that a duke had no use for Society's entertainments, but he'd spent his youth playing the role of dissolute rake to perfection and preferred never to look back.

However, the presence of Miss Lockhart was forcing him to do just that, and he didn't like what he saw.

From the corner of his eye, he caught Satterfield approaching. Titus pivoted slightly. Satterfield was one of the only people he accepted into his inner circle.

"You came," Satterfield said, echoing his wife's earlier statement.

Titus kept his focus on the street, but darted a look toward his stepfather. "You and my stepmother have so little faith in me."

"It isn't faith, my boy. It's just that we

know you." He smiled briefly. "Genie says you've been standing over here brooding the whole time."

"I'm not brooding. I'm enjoying the only company I can tolerate."

"That doesn't speak well of any of us, does it?" Satterfield said this with humor, provoking a small smile from Titus.

He glanced at his stepfather. "Present company excluded, but then you haven't been here the entire time."

"Gads no, but then I can barely tolerate this sort of thing either."

"So why are you here?"

Satterfield pivoted so that his back was to the window and he faced the room at large. "Same reason as you, I expect. I love your stepmother, and I want to support her. Did you meet Miss Lockhart?"

At the mention of her name, Titus had to reassess his behavior. Perhaps he *had* been brooding after all. "I did."

"She and Genie get on quite well. I wasn't certain this would be a good idea, but I have to admit, it seems to be working out."

Titus was glad for that—no one deserved happiness more than his stepmother. She'd accepted him as her own son the moment she'd married Titus's father and hadn't treated him any differently once she'd finally had her own child. The loss of that child, Titus's sister, was only one of the reasons Titus was eager to see her happy. He'd do anything for her, in fact. Anything except take a duchess.

Maybe someday. Just not now.

"And did your evening find a satisfying end?" Satterfield asked.

It was his polite way of asking if Titus had secured his mistress for the Season. He had. Isabelle Francis was incomparably beautiful—or so Titus had thought last night. However, she now seemed a trifle…colorless next to Miss Lockhart. Her hair was pale blond, while Miss Lockhart's was a vivid auburn. Isabelle's eyes were an incandescent blue—beautiful—but simple, as if she were only capable of a studied range of emotions. Miss Lockhart's had possessed a feral quality. Somehow he'd detected a fierce independence buried in their depths.

Titus turned his head to look at Satterfield and to see if he could catch a glimpse of Miss Lockhart. She stood on the other side of the room, engaged in conversation—a vibrant addition to the mundane tea. Indeed, she didn't look much like a companion at all. Weren't they supposed to sit out of the way and observe?

"Kendal?"

Feeling as though he'd been caught stealing a biscuit from the kitchen when he was six, he snapped his attention back to his stepfather. "Yes. Last night proved most favorable."

Today, however, was proving strange. Miss Lockhart was provoking him to feel things he hadn't in years. First was his inconvenient attraction to someone who wasn't his mistress. He hadn't been beleaguered with such nonsense in an age, and he'd be damned if he'd start now. No, that nuisance could be thwarted or at least ignored.

Second, however, was the memory of who he used to be. How, once upon a time, he might have flirted with Miss Lockhart, perhaps stolen a kiss in a dark garden, and never given her another thought.

He inwardly flinched, despising that callow young man. He caught his stepmother looking toward them meaningfully.

"Genie's giving us the evil eye," Satterfield said. "I'd best go and smooth her feathers. I'd ask you to join me, but I know what your answer will be." He clapped a hand on Titus's shoulder. "Never you mind. She's just happy you're here."

Titus watched Satterfield join the group, then turned his gaze back to the street where it was safer. However, despite his intentions, he found himself sneaking looks at Miss Lockhart several times throughout the tea.

And that simply would not do.

Chapter Three

NORA'S HEART HAD been racing at the outset of the tea this afternoon. This was her first official foray into Society, and she'd worried about how people might react when they saw her again. So far, however, things had gone swimmingly. In fact, she hadn't expected Lady Satterfield to include her quite so…robustly. As a paid companion, she'd expected to help serve tea or ensure that no one was excluded from conversation. Instead, Lady Satterfield had introduced her to everyone who arrived. It had felt—just a bit—like her first Season.

Except she was ten years older and far wiser. She hoped.

Lady Satterfield interrupted Nora's thoughts by introducing her to a new arrival, Lady Dunn. Past middle age with dark gray hair swept into an elegant style, Lady Dunn raised her quizzing glass and surveyed Nora from the top of her head to the tip of her shoe. "I remember you, gel."

Nora braced herself for what might come

next. So far no one had come out and said whether they recalled who Nora was. And Nora didn't remember Lady Dunn.

Lady Satterfield opened her mouth, but Lady Dunn spoke first. "It's good that you came back."

It was? Nora felt a surge of relief and smiled.

Lady Dunn lowered her glass. "Come and sit with me for a few minutes." She led Nora to an empty settee.

Nora glanced at Lady Satterfield, who nodded encouragingly.

Lady Dunn sat on the pale gold brocade and patted the space next to her.

Nora dropped down beside her. She had the sense Lady Dunn wanted to impart some bit of wisdom or advice.

"You're a brave young lady," Lady Dunn said without preamble. "I recall precisely what trouble you found however many years ago that was, and I can only hope you've learned your lesson."

Nora wasn't sure what to make of the woman's candor. On the one hand, it was comforting to have things out in the open, but on the other, she felt more vulnerable than she had all day. "Yes, my lady. Quite."

Lady Dunn nodded her head in one sharp bob of acknowledgment. Her gaze surveyed the room, then arrested. Her lips parted. "My goodness. The Forbidden Duke." Her tone was soft, almost breathy.

Nora followed Lady Dunn's line of sight and ended up at…the Duke of Kendal, Lady Satterfield's stepson. She looked at Lady Dunn. "The who?"

Lady Dunn blinked at Nora as if she'd grown a second head. "The Duke of Kendal. Surely you know that, since you are Lady Satterfield's companion." She pursed her lips together. "However, I suppose you wouldn't hear what's said about him from his stepmother."

Nora shouldn't want to hear what was said about him at all. She was trying to behave in the most exemplary fashion possible—no gossip, no scandal. Still, she was dying to know why he was *forbidden*.

Their brief meeting had intrigued her. He was devastatingly attractive with black hair and piercing green eyes, and he'd looked at her with…interest. Or something. There had been a hint of heat in his gaze, which she'd recognized from her experience with Haywood. She ought to run screaming in the other direction, but she sensed that he possessed something Haywood hadn't: self-control. "Why is he called that?" She immediately wished she could take the question back. She'd always been far too curious—and unable to keep her curiosity to herself.

Lady Dunn leaned forward slightly, displaying a keen interest in this topic. "Because he doesn't engage in Society, and he doesn't socialize. He holds himself apart. He isn't seen, he isn't approached, and he isn't spoken to."

He sounded like the quintessential Untouchable. She sneaked a look at him. He was tall and broad-shouldered, his thick hair waving back from his wide forehead. She could only see his profile, but his chin was square and his lips supple.

Supple?

"Why is he here, then?" Despite her brain telling her to cease pursuit of this topic, she couldn't seem to stop.

"I was hoping you could tell me, dear," Lady Dunn said with an edge of humor. "Perhaps he's on the hunt for his dance partner for Lady Satterfield's ball. It's the only event he goes to during the Season, and he always dances just once—the first dance—with a very special, and very lucky, lady."

Since Lady Dunn was so keen to share information, Nora gave up trying to quash her interest. "Special how?" she asked.

"She's invariably someone in need of attention—a spinster, a widow, the youngest daughter who's been forgotten after her elder sisters were married. His selection of her elevates her position."

He might be an Untouchable, but he sounded like a bit of a hero too.

Nora darted another look in his direction and nearly slipped off the settee. He was staring right at her, and she swore the heat in his gaze had intensified, as if he'd spent the last hour simmering over by the windows. Nora felt distinctly warm. And not uncomfortably so.

He turned his attention back to the windows, breaking their eye contact. Nora dropped her gaze and studied the small flowers on her dress in an effort to right her suddenly sideways equilibrium.

Until she'd caught him looking at her, she would've said he seemed to have no awareness of the people in the drawing room. Perhaps he should be called the Aloof Duke instead. Or maybe even the Arrogant Duke. That wasn't fair. She had no idea if he was arrogant. Perhaps he had a fear of social gatherings or people in general. Perhaps he was really the Skittish Duke. Or the Paranoid Duke. She smiled to herself, thinking she could amuse herself all day coming up with alternate names for him. The Detached Duke. Oh yes, that might fit quite nicely.

"Why are you smiling, gel?" Lady Dunn

asked.

Startled from her ridiculous reverie, Nora blinked before turning to look at Lady Dunn. "I'm just enjoying myself. Are you? Is there anything you require?"

"Not at all. It's time for me to be on my way. I should like to be the first to share the news of the Forbidden Duke's appearance, and I've several more calls to make." She held out her hand. "Help me up, dear."

Nora jumped to her feet and assisted Lady Dunn to stand. "It was a pleasure to meet you, my lady."

Even though Lady Dunn was shorter than Nora, she was somehow able to convey the effect of looking down her nose. "I'll be keeping an eye on you, Miss Lockhart. I've decided to like you. Do not disappoint me." She winked before taking herself off to bid farewell to Lady Satterfield.

Nora considered how to ask Lady Satterfield about her stepson's nickname. Later, after the tea, she'd simply tell her what Lady Dunn had said.

"Oh my goodness, is it really Miss Eleanor Lockhart?" The shrill question hit Nora's ears like a screeching falcon.

She pivoted and had to quash the look of disgust that immediately rose to her face.

Of all the people she might've chanced upon today, did it have to be Susannah Weycombe? No, she was Lady Abercrombie now. She'd been betrothed shortly after Nora had left London, and Nora had read about her lavish wedding breakfast in the newspaper.

Lady Abercrombie wasn't alone either. Another woman who'd taken great delight in Nora's disgrace, Miss Dorothy Cranley, stood beside her. At least Nora thought it was Dorothy. This woman was perhaps two stone heavier.

Nora forced a tight smile. "Good afternoon, Lady Abercrombie."

"You remember Dorothy—she's Lady Kipp-Landon now," Lady Abercrombie said.

"Yes, of course. A pleasure to see you both again." It wasn't, but Nora wouldn't say what it *really* was.

"Whatever are you doing in London?" Lady Abercrombie asked, her brown eyes wide and full to the brim with guile.

Nora inclined her head toward their hostess. "I'm companion to Lady Satterfield."

"How…charming," Lady Kipp-Landon all but sniggered. "I suppose you're just happy to be back."

Nora schooled her features into a serene

mask. Her irritation was pricked, but she wouldn't give in to it. She couldn't. "I am, thank you."

Lady Kipp-Landon edged closer to Nora. "Is that the Forbidden Duke over by the window?"

Nora wasn't sure if she was talking to her or to Lady Abercrombie, so she didn't answer.

"It *is*," Lady Abercrombie said, her tone hushed. She turned her head to Nora. "What is he doing here?"

Nora couldn't think of what to say that wasn't *It's none of your business*. She blinked at both of them and said only, "It's his stepmother's tea."

Lady Kipp-Landon fidgeted with her earring. "I've never seen him anywhere other than his stepmother's ball." She glanced at Lady Abercrombie. "Do you suppose he'll be there?" The ball was in just a few days. "And will he dance?"

Lady Abercrombie nodded gently. "I expect so. He always does. One ball. One dance. One lucky lady who never hears from him again." There was a wistfulness to her tone that wedged its way into Nora's chest.

Thankfully, Lady Satterfield looked toward her and motioned for Nora to join her. Relieved for the interruption, Nora flashed an insincere smile at the harpies. "Please excuse me."

"Certainly." Lady Abercrombie tossed a smirk at her cohort. "We wouldn't want to keep you from your duties."

Nora circuited the furniture, which took her within a few feet of the duke. He'd turned his head toward her again. She nearly tripped under the weight of his gaze. There was something palpable about his presence, as if he were a lion in his den and had become aware of the prey within his grasp.

Nonsense, she told herself. But nonsense that made her shiver nonetheless.

The remainder of the tea passed quickly, and Nora was able to keep her attention focused on the guests and not on the Forbidden Duke. Rather, *Kendal*. In fact, as the last guest departed, she turned toward the window and saw that he was gone. She'd somehow missed him leaving. Pity.

Lady Satterfield closed the door to the drawing room and exhaled. "My goodness, what a crowd today! Especially at the end."

Nora wondered if it was because word had spread that the Forbidden Duke was here.

The countess smiled at Nora. "How was it, dear? Are you exhausted?"

"Not terribly. It was a very pleasant

afternoon." Except for when her old "friends" had shown up.

"Good. I know we discussed how your past might come up, but I take it no one mentioned anything?"

"Actually, Lady Dunn was rather forthright concerning my...indiscretion."

Lady Satterfield's forehead pleated with concern. "I should have anticipated that and made sure you weren't alone with her. My apologies."

"It was fine. In fact, I rather liked her candor." Nora considered her next words carefully. "She told me Kendal is called the Forbidden Duke."

Lady Satterfield laughed, her gray eyes sparkling with mirth. "Oh yes, I imagine she did. What else did she say?"

"Only that he dances with someone special at your ball."

"Yes, he does. It's quite the *thing*."

Though Nora burned to ask why he was forbidden, she didn't dare. She'd already risked enough that afternoon and come through unscathed. Still, she could wonder how he'd earned that label. One thing was certain—he seemed a lonely figure. Did he prefer the isolation it offered, or was it a prison like Nora's own banishment had been?

She doubted she'd ever find out.

AS THE CROWD had increased toward the end of the tea, Titus had decided to take his leave. He hadn't departed the town house but had gone upstairs to his stepfather's study for a glass of brandy.

His glass was nearly empty, and he surmised from the lack of activity downstairs that the tea was now over. *Good.* He could take his leave without running into people.

Although, he might like running into Miss Lockhart.

He'd watched her as much as he dared, and a few times had caught her watching him. He'd seen her laugh and converse. She seemed charming. Witty. Probably intelligent. Or so he guessed based on her frank expression and the way she held her shoulders. Two busybodies had spoken with her, and she'd sparkled against their insipidity.

The door to the study opened and in walked his stepmother. She gave him a wide, beaming smile. "You stayed nearly the entire time."

Seeing how happy it made her was worth it.

She looked up at him eagerly. "Dare I

hope you might come again?"

"Anything's possible." But not necessarily likely. He suspected that he'd started to become a novelty toward the end of the tea—probably due to earlier guests spreading the news of his presence at their next destinations. "Are you certain you want such a crowd in future?"

His stepmother cocked her dark head to the side. "Hmm. Perhaps not." She exhaled. "Pity. You know, you could just overlook the nonsense."

He blinked at her. "I do. It's simply a nuisance, and I don't wish to beleaguer your event."

"That's very thoughtful of you, but it isn't a nuisance to me. I should endure any sort of bother if it meant you would come out of your shell a bit more."

It wasn't a shell. It was a well-guarded fortress to protect him from the absurdity of Society. He loathed the preening and the gossip and the ghastly, careless behavior. He didn't wish to discuss it further so he changed the subject. "Your new companion seemed pleasant enough." What a dull description. She was stunning and sparkled like a diamond amid coal.

"I'm quite pleased with her." Creases formed over the bridge of her nose, and Titus sensed she was about to impart

Something Important. "In fact, I'm going to ask her if she'd like to have a real Season—not just as my companion."

"What do you mean? You wish to sponsor her?"

She nodded. "I do. She was denied her chance at a happy future, and I'd like to give her a second chance."

Titus clamped his teeth together lest he speak out of turn. He didn't want her to know that he was well aware of Miss Lockhart's past—that he'd been part of the machine that had *denied* her. Yes, she'd made a mistake, but her punishment had been swift and harsh.

His stepmother continued, "I wondered if you might choose her as your dance partner at our ball."

And there it was. Every year, he danced with someone who needed a little boost in Society. It had been his stepmother's idea some six or seven years ago. It was her way to persuade him to come out from behind his wall, if only for one night, and with such a noble purpose, he'd been unable to refuse her request. In fact, it was because of Miss Lockhart that he'd agreed. He'd seen helping these specially selected women as his penance for the role he'd played in Miss Lockhart's downfall.

Now he had the opportunity to help her.

Something about the request made him feel unsettled. Why? Was it because of his involvement nine years ago? Or was it because he found her damnably attractive? None of it signified. He *owed* it to her to give her the dance.

"Consider it done."

She dropped her hand to her side, smiling. "Excellent."

"What are your intentions with regard to Miss Lockhart? Does she hope to wed?"

"I believe so. We haven't discussed it specifically. I only made my decision to offer her a Season this afternoon after watching her comport herself. You didn't ask why she needs our support, but I shall tell you anyway. She was tossed out of Society nine years ago after she was caught in an embrace with that cad Haywood." His stepmother wrinkled her nose. "She's been rusticating in the country ever since, and now her father is unable to support her. That's why she sought employment. As much as I enjoy her company—she's an excellent companion—she deserves a family of her own."

Titus could see the fire in his stepmother's eyes. As someone who'd lost her husband and her child, she took nothing for granted, and she always sought to help others. "You're an exceptionally kind person," he said softly.

"I'm just doing what any decent person would do." She straightened and pierced him with a direct stare. "Now tell me, is there any possibility you are ready to take a wife this Season?"

Titus had tossed back the last of his brandy and nearly choked. He coughed after swallowing. "I have always said that I shall when I meet a woman who is suitable."

She gave him an exasperated look. "How can you expect to meet such a person when you attend precisely one social event each year? Unless you're waiting for some girl in the Lake District to catch your fancy?"

Titus kept to himself at home as much as he did in London. If there were young ladies in the proximity of his ancestral pile, he was utterly unaware of them. The answer to her first question was that he didn't expect to meet such a person at all. "You are the one who is eager for me to wed. I see no advantage at present."

His stepmother exhaled. "No, I suppose you don't. I'm sorry to harass you, but it is my duty as your mother."

His mother.

She'd been a warm and supportive constant for most of his life, providing just the right amount of discipline and advice when he needed it. She'd been devastated by his father's death, but Titus had been utterly wrecked inside and out. He could've taken a very different path. He could've given himself over to his rakish ways and gambled or drank himself into an early grave. But he hadn't, and he had his stepmother to thank for saving him from the abyss. She hadn't blamed him for his errant ways and hadn't made him feel guilty for not realizing how serious his father's illness had been. Instead, she'd been kind and loving and had welcomed him to share in her own grief.

"Thank you," he said quietly.

She touched his arm. "I'm quite proud of you—whether you take a wife or not." She gave him the soft, gentle smile that had won him over at the age of five. "And your father would be too."

He set his empty glass on the sideboard, then bussed his stepmother's cheek. "I'll see you at the ball."

Where he would right a nine-year-old wrong and aid the woman he should have rescued. Then he could return to his ordered, mundane life, hopefully freer than he'd felt in nearly a decade.

Chapter Four
◆℈•3◆

NORA SURVEYED HERSELF in the glass, her pulse thrumming with anticipation for the ball that would shortly start downstairs. She turned to the side, admiring the drape of her gold satin gown. She looked elegant and sophisticated, and she felt beautiful for the first time in years. And she owed it all to Lady Satterfield for giving her a second chance.

Three days ago, following the tea, Lady Satterfield had surprised her by asking if she'd like to have another Season. Nora thought back to their conversation.

They'd been preparing to go to the park when Lady Satterfield had remarked upon how well Nora had navigated the tea. "You came to life," she'd said. "You ought to be more than a companion. You ought to have another Season so that you can find your rightful place, perhaps as someone's wife. If that's what you desire. Is it?"

Nora had stared at her, uncomprehending for a moment what she was asking. When she'd finally found her tongue, she'd stuttered. "Y-yes. That is, I haven't given that much thought in recent years, but yes, I'd once hoped to marry."

"Then I'll help you make that hope a reality."

"But don't you think... Don't you think it's too late? Even if I didn't have a past transgression blacking my name, I'm quite on the shelf."

Lady Satterfield had shaken her head firmly. "I do not think it's too late at all. You are very intelligent, engaging, *and* attractive. I don't think we'll have any problem finding suitors."

She'd said "we'll" as if they were a team. Nora had needed clarification. She'd had a hard time believing the countess's offer was real. "Are you going to be my sponsor?"

"Of course, dear." Lady Satterfield had smiled enthusiastically. "I'd consider it my privilege."

Nora had struggled not to cry. Lady Satterfield was the kindest person she'd met in a decade. No, she was the kindest person she'd known since her mother had died.

Tears threatened again now, and Nora blinked to keep them from falling. It wouldn't do to go downstairs with a reddened face, not when she was looking so splendid. One of the upstairs maids had performed the feat of wrestling Nora's waves into a fashionable chignon with curls framing her face. The maid had just run down to Lady Satterfield's chamber for a ribbon to complete the style. When she returned a moment later, she was accompanied by Lady Satterfield, who looked as polished as ever in a gown of burgundy edged with sleek black ribbon.

The countess brought her hand to her mouth. "Oh my goodness, you look as lovely as a princess."

Nora didn't bother containing her excitement. "That seems fitting since I feel like one."

Lady Satterfield lowered her hand, her eyes sparkling with merriment. "Well, a princess needs a bit of jewelry, don't you think? I brought you these to borrow." She held out the palm of her other hand to reveal a pair of gold filigree earrings shaped like butterflies and a matching pendant.

Nora gasped softly, again overwhelmed by the countess's thoughtfulness. "They're beautiful. Thank you."

Lady Satterfield watched as the maid fastened the necklace about Nora's neck. "Are you ready for tonight?"

"I am." Though she was nervous. What if people rejected her? The tea had gone well with only Lady Dunn mentioning her past and just the harpies treating Nora as though she didn't belong. However, a ball was something else entirely. Would anyone even ask her to dance, or would she be a wallflower? Worse, a spinster wallflower?

Well, she couldn't change the spinster part either way, since her advanced age of twenty-seven and unmarried state cast her firmly in that role. But perhaps her state was about to change. The future she'd once dreamed of—a husband and a family—was perhaps possible.

"I can't thank you enough for this opportunity," Nora said as the maid helped her with the earrings. "I find myself asking why I'm so lucky."

Finished with the jewelry, the maid moved on to looping the ribbon around Nora's head and securing it within her auburn curls. When she was finished, Lady Satterfield proclaimed her masterpiece was now complete and dismissed the maid.

Alone with Nora, Lady Satterfield gave her a wistful smile. "I had a daughter many years ago. I lost her when she was very young, so I never had the chance to watch her grow or to shepherd her through a Season. As I watched you at the tea the other day, I was struck by your charm and poise. I'd like to think my daughter would have comported herself in the same manner."

Once again, Nora found herself overcome with emotion in the face of the countess's praise. "I have no doubt, since she was your daughter." She considered adding that Lady Satterfield's daughter would never have behaved as Nora had done, but didn't want to dwell on the past. She'd done quite enough of that for nearly a decade.

"Thank you. It's silly, but even after all these years, I miss her still."

Nora didn't think it was silly at all. She felt the same about her mother. "I think the people we lose are always with us in some small way. At least that's what I like to think about my mother."

"What a lovely sentiment, my dear. I agree." Lady Satterfield turned toward the door. "Shall we go down?"

"Let's." Nora followed her from the small bedroom located on the top floor of the town house. It was a chamber for an upper servant or a child, but it was all the Satterfields had. The countess had dressed it up nicely with a comfortable four-poster bed, elegant bed hangings, a stuffed chair, and a small writing desk. There was also an armoire and, of course, the glass hanging on the wall. It made for a crowded space, but Nora had absolutely no complaints. She'd written to her sister and her father about her good fortune. Jo had been exuberantly pleased, and Nora had yet to receive a response from their father, who was apparently in the middle of moving to his sister and brother-in-law's sheep pasture.

After traipsing down two flights to the drawing room, Nora's breath caught as she stepped inside. It had been transformed into a glittering ballroom.

Doors that separated the drawing room from the smaller sitting room at the back of the house had been opened to increase the space. The furniture had been moved out that morning, and the three windows facing Mount Street were thrown open, which would allow attendees to step out onto the small balconies and take a bit of cool night air. Fresh flowers and sparkling candlelight created an atmosphere of elegance and sophistication.

The back room contained some of the furniture that had been banished from the drawing room, as well as a buffet table that would later be laden with food. For now, there was ratafia, which would be a welcome refreshment as the temperature warmed. Two sets of doors opened to the terrace that overlooked the garden below would also provide a reprieve from the heat.

Satterfield entered the drawing room then, followed by the butler, and shortly thereafter, the ball was underway. Lady Satterfield had explained that dancing would begin early in the evening. The activity would become more difficult as attendance increased and the ball became a crush. She'd also indicated that, as per custom, she and Satterfield would lead the first dance.

Over the course of the next half hour, Nora was introduced to an astonishing number of people, but had yet to receive an invitation to dance. There was still a little bit of time before the first set started. Perhaps her luck would improve.

"Eleanor!" Lady Abercrombie's high voice, coming from somewhere to the left, startled her.

Or mayhap her luck would worsen.

Nora turned slightly from her position near the back door, where she'd been enjoying the faint evening breeze. "Good evening."

Lady Abercrombie, whose blond hair was artfully woven with luminescent pearls, took in Nora's dress. Her gaze dipped, and her mouth pursed the tiniest amount, but it was enough to reveal her distaste. "I had a gown that color, my goodness when was it, two years ago?"

The subtle affront wasn't lost on Nora, but she ignored the jibe. It would take far more than that to unsettle her.

Lady Abercrombie's gaze moved past Nora, and she gasped softly. "It's him."

Nora turned as Kendal walked in from the terrace. The Forbidden Duke. He must have come up the exterior stairs to the terrace—but why enter in such a clandestine fashion?

Garbed in unrelenting black, save his snow-white cravat and shirt, he looked exactly like his nickname—an impenetrable fortress you could never hope to scale, and wouldn't even bother trying.

As with yesterday at the tea, his eyes found hers, and *now* Nora was unsettled.

But in the best possible way.

He looked at her with frank interest, his gaze burning over her with precision and then resting on her with…approval. She'd been a trifle warm, hence the reason she was standing near the doors, but now heat suffused her flesh.

"Do you know the duke?" Lady Abercrombie whispered. She stared at Nora in disbelief.

"Do you?" Nora uttered the question with a measure of sarcasm and immediately regretted it. Not because Lady Abercrombie didn't deserve it, but because

Nora knew better than to fall prey to the harpy's goading.

"I met him years ago, during my first Season. You were out at the same time, but I suppose your circle didn't extend to him." She ceased whispering. "I wouldn't have thought it would've extended to Haywood either."

Nora stiffened.

"I wonder if he'll be here tonight," Lady Abercrombie mused. "I'm sure he'll be certain to pay his respects to you." She didn't bother with sarcasm but went straight for outright malice.

Nora knew for a fact that Haywood wasn't coming, because Lady Satterfield hadn't invited him. Nora offered a bland smile and straightened, which only accentuated her height advantage over the several-inches-shorter Lady Abercrombie. "Just as I'm certain he will not be in attendance. This is a rather exclusive event, you see. In fact, I find myself wondering how you were invited. I'm confident that mistake won't be repeated."

Lady Abercrombie's nostrils flared, but before she could mount another attack, the duke swept in and offered his arm to Nora. "Miss Lockhart, I believe I have the honor of the first dance?" His deep baritone rustled over her skin like the silk of her gown when she'd donned it earlier.

"Indeed," Nora murmured, thrilled by his opportune attention. She didn't bother glancing at Lady Abercrombie as they turned toward the dance floor. Nora didn't need to see the other woman's shock in order to appreciate it.

Oh dear. She'd behaved dreadfully. Such lapses in judgment were precisely what had thrust her into trouble in the first place. And right under the Forbidden Duke's nose. "I shall apologize to Lady Abercrombie later," she said.

"Why would you do that?" he asked.

Nora blinked up at him as they made their way through the throng. It seemed to part as if by magic as they entered the drawing room. "I was rather rude. I intimated that I had a say in who Lady Satterfield invites to her ball. I must also apologize to her for my presumption."

"There won't be a need. My stepmother would applaud your response, and even if you hadn't informed that shrew that she'd no longer be welcome at Satterfield House, I would've ensured she wasn't."

Nora stared up at him. "Lady Satterfield would applaud my behavior?"

His eyes were intense, his answer equally so. "Enthusiastically. As do I."

Nora suppressed a shiver. Not only did

she have the complete support of Lady Satterfield, now she had the endorsement of the Forbidden Duke. Vindication rose within her, but she cautioned herself to keep her wits about her. However, she was finding that rather difficult in such close proximity to the attractive duke.

"We need to take our place," he said, guiding her to the dance floor, where Lord and Lady Satterfield were already at the top of the line that was forming. Kendal positioned Nora to stand beside Lady Satterfield so that they were second. The musicians, set in the far corner of the makeshift ballroom, began to play, and panic seized Nora's chest. Would she remember the steps? Would she make a fool of herself or, worse, of him?

She felt like an imposter in a scenario she'd mistakenly stumbled into. Surely someone would point her out and tell her she needed to leave. She was a pariah, an outcast. She had no place being here, let alone dancing with a *duke*.

But it was far too late to run away. The dance had started, and the line traveled the length of the drawing room. This dance would last quite some time, during which Nora would be the center of everyone's attention and the source of everyone's gossip. She could hear the exchanges now, imagined them starting up and spreading like a freshly ignited fire.

"Look at whom he chose. Who is that Nobody?"

"Don't you remember? She ruined herself nine years ago."

"How dreadful."

Lord and Lady Satterfield started, dancing their way between the lines. They were rather spry, given their age.

Nora looked nervously over at the duke. "Lady Satterfield is an excellent dancer."

"Indeed." The rich tone of his voice soothed her rioting nerves. "She always insists on calling the first, though it's the only set she'll dance."

Nora nodded. Dancing was typically reserved for the young.

She tried not to stare at her partner, but it was difficult as he was situated directly across from her and she *should* look at him. Look, yes, but not gape. And he was gape-worthy. His reputation suited him, for he *seemed* forbidden, otherworldly almost. Not in an ethereal way, but in a rustic, rough sort of manner, as if Society couldn't possibly contain him.

Despite that or perhaps because of it, he wore his costume with ease. However, she suspected he was more comfortable in riding breeches and boots as he galloped his horse across the Lake District—she'd ascertained that was where his seat was located—his powerful thighs hugging the animal's sides as they moved as one.

Goodness, where had that astonishing image come from?

And then it was their turn to traverse the line. She prayed she would remember the steps and focused on the music as they moved toward each other.

"You look as if you're headed to the guillotine," he said just loud enough for her alone to hear.

"Do I?" She tried to laugh but was afraid she sounded like a wounded bird. She longed to ask why he'd chosen her and immediately wondered if Lady Satterfield had put him up to it. She decided she didn't want to know.

"It's just a dance."

The superbly absurd comment coaxed a genuine smile to her lips and alleviated some of her discomfort. "With the 'Forbidden Duke' who only dances once each Season. Yes, you're quite right to characterize it that way. Thank you for putting me at ease."

He chuckled, and like his speaking voice, it sparked a tremor that seemed to start in her bones and move outward, making her flesh tingle and her chest warm. "Don't be nervous. And certainly don't be nervous on my account." He said the last with a tone so dry, she feared it might curl up and blow away in the breeze.

"That is easy for you, a duke, to say. I am just a simple girl who's been away from London a long time."

"I daresay you aren't 'just' anything, but I shan't debate you. Arguing in the midst of a dance is the height of boorishness."

She laughed easily this time. "Indeed it is."

He curled his arm around her waist as they passed the midpoint of the line, and they joined hands above their heads. Like his voice, his touch enthralled her, transported her to another place. A place where she wasn't a pariah or a spinster, but a woman.

When he released her hand, she felt a stab of disappointment and knew it would only deepen when he let go of her waist. But when he removed his arm, he wrapped his other one around her front and moved behind her. His gloved hand slid around her as he circled her. He came to a stop at the end of the line and faced her, his hand leaving her waist before taking her by the hand and escorting her back to her position in the line. Then he resumed his place across from her.

The move had happened quickly, but she relived it in half time—the glide of his hand, the whisper of his breath against her ear, the dark promise in his gaze when he'd faced her and taken her hand.

Silly, silly featherbrain! There was no promise—dark or otherwise. As he'd said, it *was* just a dance. A glorious, spectacular, delicious dance that she would recall at least ten thousand times.

"What do you hope to do in London this Season?" His question surprised her. She didn't know what she'd expected from someone called the Forbidden Duke, but it wasn't normal conversation.

I hope to comport myself admirably, was the first answer that came to mind, but she didn't wish to expound on that. "I imagine we'll ride in the park, pay calls, and I'll likely adorn the wall of a few dozen balls and parties." She'd meant the last in a bit of jest, but also feared it might be true.

He arched a thick brow at her. "You won't be adorning the wall. You danced with me. Everyone will want to dance with you now."

She believed him. But she also had the unsettling thought that every other partner would pale compared to him.

The next couple danced between them and joined their respective ends of the lines.

Though they were free to speak and could hear each other over the music, it meant talking at a volume that would allow their dancing neighbors to overhear. It had been one thing to converse beside his parents, but now that others could eavesdrop, she found she didn't want to say anything. Probably because the only things she wanted to discuss involved his forbidden state. How had he earned the nickname, and how did he feel about it? A shame she would never know.

At last, one of the many questions battering around in her head forced its way out. "Will you leave after our dance?" she asked, and again instantly regretted her boldness. "My apologies, that is none of my business."

"That is what I typically do, yes. However, I might linger for a bit." His gaze did just that—lingered—over her. She loved the green of his eyes, dark and mossy, almost like velvet.

The dance continued, and they exchanged a few more pleasantries. Nora was lulled into a sense of comfort, something she suspected would evaporate the moment the dance ended, which was imminent since the last couple had started down the line.

"Our dance is almost at an end," Kendal said.

"There's another in the set, is there not?"

He shook his head. "Not this time. The first set is just one dance—my stepmother prefers it that way."

Nora hadn't known this and was unaccountably disappointed. The music drew to a close, and everyone bowed or curtsied to their partner. Kendal offered his arm, and Nora clasped her hand around his sleeve. She would savor this moment, certain it would never repeat itself.

He led her back to the refreshment room, and again the throng divided as if by some sort of spell. But then it seemed Kendal excelled at casting a very specific sort of magic that drove everyone into an obsequious state.

They happened upon Lady Dunn, who was seated near the wall. Her gaze fell on them with something akin to admiration or maybe approval. Kendal took his leave, and Lady Dunn motioned for Nora to join her.

"Well done, my dear," the older woman said. "When next we meet—away from this crush—you must recount the entire dance. I want to hear every single detail, beginning with why he asked you."

That was a question Nora didn't have an answer to and would forever ponder—

when she wasn't too busy just feeling happy
that he had.

Chapter Five

HAVING DONE HIS duty to his stepmother, Titus went upstairs to Satterfield's study to escape the inanity of the ball goers. *Not all of them were tedious*, he told himself. One in particular was quite intriguing.

He heard a steady stream of women accessing his stepmother's sitting room next door, which had been converted into a retiring room. He wondered if any of them were Miss Lockhart with her gold-brown eyes and alluring smile.

His annual dance had always been a duty, but tonight he'd enjoyed performing it more than he ever had. Miss Lockhart was refreshingly open. He'd had to keep from laughing aloud at the way in which she'd put that ridiculous carper in her place. He hadn't felt so at ease with another person who wasn't from his inner circle in a very long time. In forever, maybe.

And just who was his "inner circle"? His stepmother, of course, and Satterfield. His steward at Lakemoor, his secretary here in London, probably his valet, and perhaps his butlers. Maybe the stable master at Lakemoor. Once upon a time, he would've included the group of friends he'd run with in his youth, but he'd left them behind when he'd shunned their lifestyle. Some of them had matured a bit, while others were as debauched as ever. He was friendly with a few of them—they discussed politics and the like—but he didn't socialize with them.

Hmm, yes, he was alone, but not lonely, as his stepmother surmised, and he liked it that way.

As if he'd summoned her by thought, the door opened and Lady Satterfield walked inside, saying, "There you are. Harley said you hadn't left, which I could scarcely believe."

Titus had conversed briefly with the Satterfields' butler before coming upstairs. Just as he'd been surprised by Titus's arrival at the tea the other day, he'd seemed taken aback to learn that Titus wasn't leaving as soon as he'd completed the favor for Lady Satterfield.

Titus shrugged and sipped from the glass of whisky he'd poured from his stepfather's cabinet. "I just needed some quiet."

"Do you mean to return to the ball?" she asked, with perhaps a touch of hope.

He shrugged again.

She shook her head but smiled. "You

needn't stay. I appreciate you dancing with Nora."

Nora. He tried to think of her as Miss Lockhart, but from the moment he'd heard her name and experienced the sensuality it seemed to spark in his brain, he'd had a rough go of it. Maybe he'd abandon the pretense—at least in his head.

"Did it help?" he asked.

His stepmother exhaled. "I'm not sure yet. She's just received her second invitation to dance, and Lady Dunn, bless the woman despite her penchant for gossip, has given her stamp of approval." Her lips curved down. "However, there are other women—who I think knew Nora in the past—who have not been as gracious."

Titus felt an urge to return to the ball and glower at the termagant who'd been bothering Nora. "Yes, I overhead one of them speaking to Miss Lockhart. I don't know her name, but ask Miss Lockhart. You mustn't ever invite her to Satterfield House again."

His stepmother arched a brow at him. "Indeed? You sound as if you leapt to her defense."

Titus didn't want to expose his guilt regarding Nora or the fact that he felt beholden to help her. "I am doing what you asked—elevating her status."

"And I appreciate it. Perhaps then you won't mind lending just a bit more of your support. We're to attend Lady Fitzgibbon's picnic at Brexham Hall in a few days. Will you join us?"

Titus couldn't think of anything he'd rather do less. The thought of spending an entire afternoon at an insipid Society event made his skin crawl. Once upon a time, he'd enjoyed such nonsense, but now he'd rather meet with his secretary or dig into a treatise or a book.

However, this event would include Nora. Surely that would lift its potential from certainly dull to possibly entertaining?

"You needn't come for the entire time," his stepmother said. "Hopefully by then she will have garnered a bit of favor, perhaps even a potential suitor or two, and your continued attention will only solidify her status."

Of course there would be suitors. She was looking for a husband, was she not? Still, the thought of a gentleman courting her inexplicably provoked his irritation. "I will put in an appearance. Will that suffice?"

Her brows climbed into a graceful arch of surprise. "More than. I expected you to say no."

If it had been anyone other than Nora,

he would have. But he felt a specific responsibility to aid her cause. He may not have been the one to compromise her, but he may as well have been standing there encouraging Haywood.

"Perhaps you're finally letting down your guard." His stepmother lifted a shoulder and gave him a sly smile. "Who knows, maybe you'll even take a wife."

"Let's not put the cart before the horse." He tossed back the rest of his whisky.

She chuckled. "Never. And anyway, I'm quite content playing sponsor to Miss Lockhart. Once I've secured her future, I may take on another young lady. It's quite invigorating." Her smile was tinged with sadness. "It makes me think of Eliza."

She was speaking of Titus's half sister who'd died at the age of three, when Titus had been ten. There had been no other children after that, so it made sense that helping Nora appealed to her. He set his empty glass on the sideboard and took his stepmother's gloved hand. "I'm sorry this is dredging that up."

She squeezed his fingers and let him go. "I'm not. And anyway, there is no dredging involved. Eliza is always with me." She briefly touched her chest above her heart before tugging her glove more snugly over her elbow. "I do worry about you, though.

Are you truly happy on your own?"

"As happy as I need to be." He would've said *as I deserve to be*, but that would have invited unwanted questions and concern. "I shall be happier in a short while when I am away from this ball." Indeed, why hadn't he left already?

An image of Nora—the proud angle of her head and the confident jut of her chin as she'd put that woman in her place—rose in his mind, and he silently chided himself. He'd wasted a perfectly good hour—more than that now—that he could've spent at his club or in his library. Or better yet, in the arms of his mistress.

His stepmother walked toward the door. "I'm afraid I must return downstairs. I've been gone an age." She paused at the threshold. "Will you come with me, or are you leaving?"

"Leaving."

"Good night, then." She blew him a kiss and left.

Titus followed her from the room, but as he escaped down the back stairs, he wondered if he'd really go to his mistress. He hadn't been to see her since that first night, what, nearly a week ago? The night before he'd met Nora.

Clenching his jaw, he resolved to visit Isabelle. He needed to return to his normal

London routine, which included regular appointments with his mistress. But as he climbed into his coach, he wasn't thinking of his beautiful courtesan. No, he was thinking of tawny eyes and dark pink lips that belonged to a woman he could never have.

❦

TWO NIGHTS LATER, Nora attended a soiree with Lady Satterfield at the home of Lord Bunting. It wasn't a crush, but there was far more of a crowd than Nora had anticipated. She'd forgotten how many people spent their evenings seeking entertainment around London. It made the last nine years of her life seem incredibly sedate and painfully lonely.

But then she hadn't needed the social whirl of London to underscore that point.

She'd been too aware of her solitude as well as the fact that she'd be alone forever. Until she wasn't. And now that she wasn't… Well, it felt strange to be thrust into this madness again.

Madness? Was that how she saw it?

Yes, because *anyone* would acknowledge that the London Season was overwhelming and terrible and quite, quite mad.

Then why was she here?

Because she didn't want to go back to the way things were—not that she could, given her father's failures. Still, she didn't have to be doing *this*. She could content herself with working as someone's companion. Except the temptation of a husband, a family, of a quiet, comfortable life was too great to ignore.

"Nora?" Lady Satterfield interrupted Nora's woolgathering in the saloon, where the women had moved after dinner.

Nora realized she'd missed whatever conversation had been going on around her and silently chided herself to pay more heed. She didn't want to embarrass Lady Satterfield. "I was just wondering when the dancing might start," she said, in an effort to mask her inattention.

Lady Satterfield's brow made a tiny crease, but only for a fleeting moment. "Lady Bunting just indicated the drawing room is ready. Shall we go?"

As the other women began to rise, Nora inwardly cringed at having been caught fibbing. She stood, and Lady Satterfield leaned close. "It's quite all right. If you're tired, we can make an early night of it."

Nora wanted to hug the countess for her quick and compassionate understanding. But she wasn't tired. She was just… She didn't know what she was. Eager to dance, she decided. Yes, that was one thing about London she loved and felt fortunate to take part in once again.

"Thank you, but I'd like to stay. I simply became lost in my thoughts for a few minutes." Nora left the sitting room at Lady Satterfield's side.

As soon as they entered the drawing room, Nora was beset by a trio of gentlemen who asked her to dance. She promised to partner all three of them, and they took their leave until the music started.

Lady Satterfield beamed at her. "My goodness, that was wonderful, wasn't it?"

Nora didn't know what to say. After dancing with Kendal the other night, she'd danced just twice more. She'd appreciated the attention but had assumed it was because she was the ward of the hostess. Tonight, however, she was simply another guest. And perhaps a sought-after one at that.

After so many years away and because of the manner in which she'd left town, she couldn't help but feel wary. She turned to Lady Satterfield. "Why do you suppose that happened?"

Lady Satterfield let out a light laugh. "You are attractive, intelligent, and beyond the age of simpering. I imagine that will appeal to a great many gentlemen."

Nora wondered if the modest dowry, which Lord and Lady Satterfield had insisted on settling on her, had also played a part. Probably, but that was how things worked. One married for a variety of reasons, including financial gain. Wasn't Nora looking to improve her own station? She wasn't in search of a title or an excess of money, but she *did* desire comfort.

Her first partner was Lord Markham, an earl in his middle thirties with a fading hairline and a warm smile. He'd spent the past decade serving the government and was now, according to Lady Satterfield, on the hunt for a wife.

They spoke of London entertainments and outdoor pursuits. He was an affable fellow, and Nora enjoyed their time together. But it was over soon enough, and she went on to her next partner, Mr. Reginald Dawson. As with the first dance, she and Mr. Dawson exchanged pleasantries. A bit younger than Lord Markham, Dawson was a widower with two small children. He made no secret of saying he was looking for a new wife—one who wouldn't shrink from stepping into the role of mother.

"I suspect I'm in for a challenge," he said. "Trying to find a lady who won't mind an immediate family." He glanced at Nora as the dance drew to an end.

Nora thought about that—an instant family—and decided it didn't frighten her. She had next to no experience with children, but she wasn't afraid of the prospect, not when she heartily wanted a family of her own. "Oh, I don't know," she said, taking his arm so that he could lead her from the dance floor. "You might be surprised, Mr. Dawson."

He shot her a glance that was, in fact, surprised, his dark brown eyes sparkling. "Indeed? That is excellent to hear."

Dawson guided her to the refreshment table, where Nora accepted a glass of ratafia.

"Thank you again for the dance," Dawson said, his lips curving into a smile. "I shall look forward to our next encounter." He presented a gallant bow, to which Nora responded with a curtsey.

As soon as he left, a woman approached, and Nora nearly choked on her drink. It was Lady Kipp-Landon, with whom she'd become reacquainted at Lady Satterfield's tea.

Nora eyed the other woman with a healthy sense of caution and glanced around for her companion, the supercilious Lady Abercrombie. Thankfully, she was nowhere to be seen.

Lady Kipp-Landon stretched her lips into a ghastly smile. Or at least it looked ghastly to Nora. Something about it didn't ring quite true. Maybe it was because of what she said. "How delightful to see you here, Miss Lockhart. What a lovely gown." Her gaze dipped to Nora's costume, which was a paler shade of the gold she'd worn to Lady Satterfield's ball—a color Lady Abercrombie had mocked.

The devil nestled close on Nora's shoulder. "You're sure the color isn't too outdated?" she asked and almost instantly regretted it. She mustn't sink to their level.

Lady Kipp-Landon's eyes widened briefly. "Oh no, not at all! It's quite fetching on you. I see you danced with Lord Markham." She sidled closer to Nora as if they were friends. "Does he plan to call on you?"

For a moment, Nora simply stood there and tried to make sense of what was happening. Did Lady Kipp-Landon *think* they were friends?

"I'm sure I don't know," Nora murmured. "If you'll excuse me, I need to find the retiring room."

"Of course. It's upstairs—you can't miss it." Her face brightened. "Lovely to chat with you. Mayhap we'll see each other in the park tomorrow!"

Nora couldn't help but look at the woman as if she'd sprouted a third ear. She'd seen Lady Kipp-Landon and Lady Abercrombie in the park the day after Lady Satterfield's ball and they hadn't said a word to her. What had changed?

She went to the retiring room and was fortunate to run into Lady Satterfield, who pulled her aside. "How is your evening?"

"Fine, thank you. I just danced with Mr. Dawson."

"Ah yes. How was it?"

"Quite pleasant." Nora had hesitated in her answer, but not because of her dance with Dawson. She was still thinking of Lady Kipp-Landon's peculiar behavior.

Lady Satterfield looked at Nora intently, perhaps detecting her lingering unease. She lowered her voice and turned her back to the retiring room. "Is there something else?"

Nora glanced around the room. Aside from an older woman seated on a chaise near the corner, it was empty. "Lady Kipp-Landon spoke with me...as if we were friends."

Lady Satterfield frowned. "What did she say?"

"She asked about Lord Markham, complimented my gown, and said she looked forward to seeing me in the park."

Lady Satterfield was aware of how she and Lady Abercrombie had behaved toward Nora, especially the latter at Lady Satterfield's ball. As promised, Kendal had mentioned something to his stepmother, and now Lady Abercrombie was forever banned from the countess's invitation list.

Lady Satterfield's gray eyes lit. "I see what's happening. Lady Kipp-Landon recognizes that you are becoming popular. You've attracted the notice of several gentlemen, including an earl. She'd do better to have you as an ally than an enemy."

Nora shook her head in disgust. "But it's all so affected. She doesn't actually *want* to be my friend."

"Perhaps not," Lady Satterfield said gently. "And you needn't befriend her, of course. However, I would urge you to be pleasant, as it will only help your cause."

So Nora would have to resort to deceit as well if she wanted to achieve her goal of finding a husband. She'd known, even in her youth, that one must put on a performance of sorts to gain acceptance and attract suitors. But now that she was older, she wasn't at all sure she *wanted* to do those things. Her feelings of unease didn't dissipate.

Lady Satterfield frowned slightly. "You

still seem diffident. Is there anything I can do?"

Nora didn't want to concern her. "No, I'm just out of practice."

The countess brightened. "Of course you are. It's quite a change of pace. You mustn't worry about feeling overwhelmed or unsure. You'll find your footing again, you'll see." Lady Satterfield touched her arm. "But if you want to leave any event ever, you need only say the word. Your well-being is my priority, dear."

Nora smiled at her kind benefactress. "You are surely heaven-sent."

Lady Satterfield laughed. "I'm not certain my husband or stepson would agree with you."

"Nonsense. They both adore you." Or so it seemed to Nora.

"Yes, but that doesn't mean I don't try their patience from time to time." She winked at Nora. "Come, I'll wait for you while you tidy up, and we'll head back down. You've another dance scheduled, do you not?"

Nora nodded. She conducted a brief toilette, then they returned to the party. As Nora began her next dance, she hoped that what Lady Satterfield said was true—that she'd become comfortable soon. However, the alternative, that she simply didn't like this life, loomed in the forefront of her mind.

Maybe she'd be fortunate enough to find a husband who would provide a quieter country life as she'd become accustomed to. Perhaps someone like Mr. Dawson. Definitely not an Untouchable like the Duke of Kendal. That had been her ambition during her first Seasons, the sparkling dream that she'd foolishly thought was in her grasp.

This time she understood the possibilities, as well as the stakes. And she didn't plan to fall victim to Society's vagaries again.

Chapter Six

BREXHAM HALL, THE London residence of Lord Fitzgibbon, was a century-old country house of Palladian design set upon some five hundred acres. Its grandeur and proximity to town made it a favorite haven of the ton. As such, Titus had been here only a handful of times, and never for Lady Fitzgibbon's annual picnic.

A receiving line of sorts had been established along the path as people made their way toward the picnic, and the Satterfields—and Nora—were just concluding a short exchange with their hosts. Titus had ridden his horse to the picnic and gone directly to the stables, and now avoided the receiving line.

Nora cocked her head to the side, a wide-brimmed bonnet shading her face from both the bright sunlight and him. No matter, for he could recall the slope of her nose, the generous sweep of her lower lip, and the warm sparkle in her tawny eyes. Those very features had haunted his dreams. When he considered the cause, he blamed the guilt he felt. Hopefully today's errand would set him free.

As they departed the line and continued along the path, Titus made his way in their direction. He was vaguely aware of people staring at him as he passed. He hadn't attended this many Society events—the tea, the ball, and now this—in such quick succession, since before his father had died.

His stepfather caught sight of him first and inclined his head as he bent to say something to Titus's stepmother.

She turned to greet him. "Ah, Kendal, I'm delighted to see you here." She angled her head toward Nora. "Look who's come, Nora."

Nora turned and tipped her head up. Her warm brown eyes, so bold and expressive, charmed him. "Good afternoon, Your Grace."

He took her hand and pressed his lips to the back of her glove. The garment offended him because he would rather have kissed her bare flesh. "Good afternoon. It's a nice day for a picnic."

The inane comment sounded absurd to his ears. He hadn't tried to make such nonsensical chitchat in ages.

His stepmother smiled widely. "It's especially fine today. I don't remember the last time Lady Fitzgibbon's annual picnic was blessed with such lovely weather. Kendal, come and join us at our blanket." She took her husband's arm and led the way.

Titus held his arm for Nora. She curled her hand around his sleeve, and Titus's body came alive with awareness. Damn.

He strove to keep his mind away from her charms. "I understand you're keeping my stepmother busy."

Nora cast him an enigmatic look—it was almost inquisitive, and yet she didn't ask a question. "We've been adding to my wardrobe. She's been incredibly generous. She says it gives her pleasure to have a young woman to support and shepherd." She shook her head, her lips curving in a self-deprecating half smile. "I only wonder what I did to earn such kindness." Ah, *that* was her question: why her?

Because she deserved it.

"Does it have to be something that you did?" Titus asked. "My stepmother is an exceptionally benevolent person by nature. I'm not the least bit surprised that she wanted to sponsor you."

They crested a small hill, and the picnic lay before them. Dozens of colorful blankets set as elegantly as a Society dinner dotted the verdant lawn. The thought of sharing Nora with a blanketful of people annoyed him nearly as much as the glove on her hand. Which was ridiculous. He was here to ensure her acceptance and success. He had no personal interest or stake other than righting the wrong he'd done her.

He sought to keep the conversation benign. He'd once been very good at charming young ladies with his conversational wit. In retrospect, that seemed like another life. "Have you been to Brexham Hall before?"

She looked at him askance, and her expression was tinged with disbelief. "Goodness no. I wasn't in a high enough position during my Seasons. Brexham Hall is a destination for the Untouchables."

"What the devil are the Untouchables?"

She laughed, and he loved the dark, throaty sound of it. "Spoken like a true Untouchable." She looked at him again, this time studying him at length. "Shall I explain?"

"No, I think I comprehend the meaning." He tried not to scowl. This sharp division even among the upper class was another reason he'd come to loathe Society. He didn't care for other people dictating whom he ought to befriend or associate with. Or dance with. Or fall in love with.

Not that he was in danger of *that*.

"I didn't mean to offend you," she said softly.

She hadn't, but he acknowledged he wasn't exhibiting his best side to her. Hell, did he even have a *good* side? He'd long ago abandoned comporting himself in the manner necessary to win smiles and affection, and back when he had, the skill had come effortlessly. What had happened to him in the intervening years? He knew: a persistent feeling of disgust from his youthful behavior and a heavy dose of cynicism engendered by the very people he'd once called "friends."

Nora, however, was not one of those people. She was someone with whom he could relax and let down his guard—if he wanted to.

He studied her pert profile.

Yes, he wanted to, but he wouldn't. There was no point when their association would be disappointingly brief.

"It is I who must apologize. I'm afraid I don't socialize well," he said.

"You did fine at your stepmother's ball."

He sent her a wry glance. "I've had enough practice with that particular occasion—that's the one thing I do annually, if you recall."

She laughed again, and the sound burrowed into him, sparking something most inconvenient—*desire*. "I do recall, and even if I didn't, there are plenty who will remind me."

He couldn't help but join in her mirth. "That is true. It's an appalling state."

She adjusted her hold on his arm, sending a shock of awareness straight to his gut. "People talking about you?"

"I don't much care if people talk about me. As you so aptly stated, I am untouchable. Most, however, are not. I find gossip and the proclivity of much of Society to burrow their noses in other people's business abhorrent."

Her gaze took on a sheen of approval. "You're most vehement."

"As any full-witted person ought to be."

She pressed her lips together, and he had the sense she was trying not to grin. "I agree."

He allowed his lips to curve into a smile. "Of course you do."

She'd already demonstrated her keen intelligence and delicious wit the other night. She was, so far, unlike any other young lady he'd met.

Her eyes narrowed in a playful, almost flirtatious manner. "Your Grace, I think you *do* know how to socialize. You flatter me."

Apparently   he   hadn't   completely

forgotten how. "Only by chance."

"Oh? You didn't mean to be complimentary?" Definitely flirtatious, judging by her arch tone.

He couldn't help but warm to her vivacity. "See? I told you I wasn't good at this. I didn't set out to charm you. I don't set out to charm anyone." Not anymore.

"And that's precisely what I find so…charming," she murmured, her eyes glowing like dark amber.

They'd traversed the path to the site of the picnic and now made their way to their assigned blanket. This area was flat, but past the picnic area, the ground gently sloped down toward the small lake, where a handful of boats bobbed near the shoreline. A group of footmen stood at the ready to assist picnickers into the watercrafts.

Nora gestured toward the lake. "Oh, there are boats!" Her unabashed glee coaxed another smile to his lips.

His stepmother turned upon hearing Nora's exclamation. "Indeed. We shall see if we can persuade Mr. Dawson to take you out in one." She gave her ward a mischievous grin.

Dawson? Who the hell was Dawson?

Titus had almost forgotten that the goal was to give Nora a Season, and more importantly, the chance to find the husband that she was denied. He'd been about to offer to take her onto the lake himself, but it was better that she went with someone else. Someone she could marry. He was *not* that someone. A wife would intrude on the solitude he loved, but more than that, Nora wouldn't want him—not after he'd contributed to her disgrace.

His stepmother looked at him with satisfaction in her gaze. "He danced with Miss Lockhart last night. As did several other gentlemen. Miss Lockhart is becoming quite popular."

Nora blushed and didn't meet Titus's gaze. "I hardly think so."

A scowl sprang to Titus's mouth, but he was able to wrestle it into a mere grimace. Then he forced himself to smile. Again. "How nice."

"Shall we sit?" his stepmother asked.

Titus reluctantly withdrew his arm from Nora's electrifying touch. "I'm not staying."

Nora's gaze snapped to his, her disappointment evident. "You aren't?"

His stepmother gave him a cross look. "I was hoping you might stay longer." Her eyes narrowed, and he knew a discussion would be forthcoming—either now or later.

His stepfather intervened, but not in the way Titus would have hoped. "Come, Miss

Lockhart, let us sit down." He guided her to the blanket.

Titus's stepmother pulled him a discreet distance from the blankets and, more importantly, from inquisitive ears. Clearly the interview was to come now. "Can't you stay a little while?"

"Why? You have this Dawson chap on leading strings already, do you not? Plus any number of other gentlemen. I've done what I said I would."

She studied him with a small frown. "You seem annoyed. Do you have a problem with Dawson?"

Hell. He didn't even know the man. He only knew the thought of him—of *anyone*—courting Nora was akin to a splinter stuck beneath his thumbnail. "I'm sure Dawson is splendid." He made an effort not to grit his teeth.

She peered at him expectantly. "Is there any possibility *you* might be interested in Miss Lockhart?"

Interested. That word could encompass many things. Did he want to converse with her about such inanities as the weather and the color of the ocean? Yes. Did he wish to dance with her or take her out in a dinghy on a tiny lake? Yes and yes. Did he desire the heat of her gaze upon him, the touch of her hand, the press of her lips against his?

Holy hell, yes.

He looked over at her sitting next to his stepfather on the blanket. He could almost smell her lilac scent.

"No," he said tightly, thinking that the constrained sound of that single word somehow approximated the feel of his breeches around his thickening cock. It was past time to leave.

His stepmother's answering look indicated she didn't entirely believe him, but he didn't care to debate the point. "Well, if you were, I would endorse your suit."

Of course she would. She wouldn't care if Titus wished to court a washerwoman or a princess. She only wanted him to be happy. And that was why he loved her.

"I'm leaving now." He took a step toward the path.

"Will you come for dinner later?" she asked.

During the Season, he typically had dinner with them once a week or so. But that was when it had just been the three of them. Now there was Nora, to whom he was apparently insanely attracted. "I don't know. I have some things to read."

She rolled her eyes but smiled too. "You always do. I hope we'll see you. You know you're always welcome."

He chanced another glance at Nora and had the air sucked straight from his lungs when he saw she was looking right at him. Those inquisitive, gorgeous eyes of hers seemed as though they might pierce directly into his soul, if he let them.

And he wouldn't. Of all the women he might finally allow into his life, she was the one he couldn't consider. She was the one who'd eviscerate him if she ever discovered the role he'd played in her downfall—and rightly so.

Chapter Seven
❧❧

NORA CLUTCHED THE side of the small boat as it teetered precariously.

Mr. Dawson laughed warmly. "I've got it now, I think." They'd been in the boat ten minutes, and he was having the devil of a time figuring out how to row properly. Nora feared they were going to end up swimming in the small lake.

The craft evened out, and Nora loosened her grip, though she kept one hand on the side. Why, she didn't know. It wasn't as if holding on to the boat would save her from a dunking if they tipped over. She wondered if Kendal would've had such trouble and instantly doubted it. His entire demeanor suggested he commanded everything he did. He wouldn't allow a small watercraft to be a nuisance.

She looked over at Mr. Dawson, with whom she'd danced last night. He was a pleasant fellow perhaps five years her senior. A widower, he was on the hunt for a wife—and a mother for his two children back in Sussex. He seemed an affable sort, quick to laugh and charm, with an ever-ready smile lighting his acorn-brown eyes.

His light brown wavy hair fell across his forehead, and he pushed it back as he fought to turn the boat back toward the dock. "My apologies, Miss Lockhart. I'm afraid I'm not much of a sportsman. However, if you desire an engaging chess match or game of cards, I'm your fellow."

Nora worked to ignore the rocking of the boat. She'd suffered worse during their short jaunt, but she'd feel much better when they were back on land. "As a matter of fact, I enjoy chess immensely. My father taught me to play when I was younger." Before he'd withdrawn into himself after Mother had died.

Mr. Dawson inclined his head. "Excellent. I look forward to playing with you some time."

That he spoke of some future activity surprised Nora. Did that mean he was interested in courting her? She was woefully out of practice when it came to this game. If she'd ever been any good at it. One could argue she was an abject failure at husband hunting.

They were headed toward another craft. Nora put both hands on the sides again as she tensed. "Careful of the other boat," she said, perhaps stating the obvious. However, she wanted to be certain Mr. Dawson saw them.

He dug the oar deeper into the water as he worked to alter their course. "Yes, I see them. This is just so…difficult." He grimaced as he barely managed to divert the boat. The man rowing the other boat had acted quickly and was probably the reason they'd avoided a glancing collision.

As it was, the two crafts came abreast of each other and exchanged friendly waves. Nora overheard what the woman in the other boat said to her companion, "Did you see the Forbidden Duke? Lady Faversham said he was here, but I didn't see him."

"I did not, but I daresay she was mistaken," the gentleman replied. "He doesn't attend gatherings like this."

"That's what I said. But she was most insistent."

Nora didn't say a word as the growing distance between them prevented her from hearing any more of their conversation.

Mr. Dawson let his hands go slack with the oars hovering above the surface of the water. "We are approaching land at last." He flashed her a self-deprecating smile. "You must be terribly relieved."

"Will you dislike me if I say I am?"

He laughed. "Heavens, no, I shall respect

your honesty."

The boat tapped the dock, and a footman helped them to disembark.

Once Nora's feet were safely on the ground, she fully relaxed, giving her shoulders a little shake as the tension seeped from them. She turned to Mr. Dawson, who was adjusting his hat. "This is much better," she said.

"Agreed." He offered her his arm, and they strolled back toward her blanket. "I think I shall keep my feet on terra firma from now on. Unless someone else is steering the boat."

"An excellent notion."

He cast her a quick glance. "I hope you managed to enjoy yourself despite my ineptitude."

"I had a lovely time—you are not inept. You acquitted yourself far better than I would have."

"Only because you haven't practiced."

"And you have?" she asked, looking at him askance.

He chuckled. "Not really. Perhaps you *would* have done better."

They arrived at Nora's blanket, and she thanked him again for the boat ride.

Lady Satterfield put her hand at the edge of her bonnet brim for additional shade as she looked up at them. "Did you enjoy yourselves?"

"Yes, quite," Nora said as she sat down beside her.

Mr. Dawson executed a bow. "Until next time, Miss Lockhart." As he straightened and turned, his toe caught the edge of Lady Satterfield's plate, flipping it so the contents, including a large dollop of jam, landed against Nora's skirt.

His face creased with distress. "Oh no! I am absolutely graceless. My sincerest apologies."

Lady Satterfield dabbed at Nora's skirt with a napkin. "You should get some water on that."

Nora's dress, like her entire wardrobe, was new. She didn't want to think it might be ruined, not after the trouble and expense Lady Satterfield had gone to. She also didn't want Mr. Dawson to feel bad. She smiled brightly up at him. "It's quite all right. Accidents happen all the time. I once spilled an entire glass of ratafia down my front." During her first Season. It had ruined the ball gown, much to her cousin's dismay. "I'll just take a quick trip to the retiring room."

Mr. Dawson offered his hand to help her up.

"I'll come with you, dear," Lady Satterfield said, and Mr. Dawson also assisted her to stand.

"I do hope you won't think poorly of me after this," Mr. Dawson said earnestly.

Nora smiled at him. "Of course not."

He offered another bow—causing no damage this time—and took his leave. Nora departed with Lady Satterfield toward the house.

"I daresay a courtship might be in the offing," Lady Satterfield said when they were out of earshot of the blanket.

"We scarcely know each other." For some reason, Nora thought of Kendal. She scarcely knew him either, and yet he occupied so many of her thoughts. She wished he hadn't left the picnic.

Lady Satterfield started up the short set of stairs to the back patio. "I've been around a long time, and I'd say Dawson is definitely interested in you. He danced with you last night and sought you out today. That's interest."

Again, Nora's mind summoned Kendal. He'd *also* danced with Nora, and he'd also sought her out today. Perhaps the latter wasn't precisely true—she had no evidence that he'd come to the picnic in order to see her. Really, that would be absurd. But why had he come, particularly when it was common knowledge that he didn't, as a general rule?

Why did her thoughts keep going back to Kendal? Was it because he'd been the first to pay her attention or because he was…Kendal?

What does that even mean?

It meant he was extraordinary. Definitive. The Forbidden Duke. Whether he'd come to the picnic to see her or not, he'd paid her special attention—not this once, but *twice*. The realization sent a delicious shiver up her spine. She'd thought they might've shared a connection at Lady Satterfield's ball, probably because of the way he'd looked at her at Lady Satterfield's tea—as if he'd wanted to know her.

You are being entirely ridiculous.

Just because he made her heart race and he'd been nice to her on a pair of occasions didn't mean he wanted anything more than an acquaintance. He was the Forbidden Duke—he wasn't interested in anyone. He was likely only paying her attention because Lady Satterfield had taken her in.

"Does Mr. Dawson interest you?" Lady Satterfield's query drew Nora from her fanciful thoughts. "He's not wealthy, but I believe he's comfortable enough. And he does have children, so you'd have to become an instant mother." Her features softened. "I've done that myself, of course, and it's wonderful."

With Kendal. She'd become his mother when she'd married his widowed father. That much Nora had learned in the days since she'd moved to Lady Satterfield's town house.

Nora didn't think before saying the next thought that crossed her brain. "I heard someone talking about Kendal on the lake." She cast Lady Satterfield a worried glance. She hadn't meant to gossip, especially about the woman's own son. Oh, she was worse than out of practice. She was hopeless. "My apologies. I shouldn't repeat such things."

Lady Satterfield laughed. "It's hard to ignore talk about my stepson. Especially at an event like this."

They reached the door to the house, and Nora followed Lady Satterfield into the drawing room. "Surely he should be able to attend a picnic without scrutiny?"

Lady Satterfield lifted a shoulder. "This is London, dear. An unmarried duke can't do anything without scrutiny."

"Lady Satterfield!" An older woman strode toward them. "I must speak with you. Is it true Kendal was here earlier? Is he finally on the hunt for a wife?"

Lady Satterfield turned to Nora. "Do you require assistance in the retiring room? It's just through there down the corridor." She gestured toward a doorway.

"No, I'll be fine." She suppressed a smile. "I'll leave you to deal with…that."

Lady Satterfield's eyes sparkled with mirth as she whispered, "This could be fun."

Nora had no idea what Lady Satterfield intended to say or do to make that encounter "fun," but imagined she'd hear all about it later. She found the retiring room with ease and tended to the spot on her skirt. The outline of the stain was still there, but with treatment when they returned home, it would be salvageable.

She found herself in a strange room and realized she'd taken a wrong turn out of the retiring room. She spun on her heel and was about to retrace her steps when her heart lodged in her throat. There, blocking the doorway, was Lord Haywood, the very last person she ever wanted to see, never mind encounter alone.

He was as tall as she remembered, but he'd filled out a bit so that he didn't seem as athletic as he'd been in her memory. And his pale hair was thinning. But his cobalt eyes were as vivid and alluring as ever. Those eyes had seduced her, along with the smile that was currently curving his thin lips.

Had she really found him devastatingly

attractive once? Now he seemed utterly lacking, especially when compared with Kendal, the man who had somehow become Nora's measuring stick for all other men.

The tension she'd felt on the lake returned tenfold as she searched for another way out of the small sitting room. There was another door, but she had no idea where it led. For all she knew, it was a closet and she'd be even more trapped than she already was.

"Miss Lockhart?" His deep voice rattled her already screaming nerves. "I had heard you were back in town. I'm so glad we've run into each other." He crossed the room toward her, leaving the doorway accessible—provided she could get around him.

She knew she ought to be polite, perhaps act as though she didn't even know him. But the pain and injustice of nine years surged through her. "I would prefer it if you never spoke to me." She forced herself to move and made to barrel past him.

He snagged her elbow, drawing her to a stop near his side. He pivoted without releasing her. "There's no call to be rude. I only wanted to say how lovely you look. It seems the country agrees with you."

"Don't you mean banishment?" she

snapped. She wrenched her arm free and took a large step away from him. "I have nothing to say to you. Ever."

"Pity, for I'd hoped we might rekindle our acquaintance." His gaze raked her in a manner that left no doubt as to what he meant by "acquaintance."

She stared at him in disbelief. "You're disgusting. And married. I ought to tell your wife."

He laughed. "Tell her what? That you cornered me in a sitting room again? I imagine that will work out quite well for you a second time."

"Go to the devil." Nora resisted the urge to slap his smug face before she whirled about and stalked from the room.

She hurriedly made her way back to Lady Satterfield, passing the retiring room just as the door opened—and out walked Lady Abercrombie, whom Nora careened into.

Lady Abercrombie stepped back from her and brushed at her arm where they'd collided. "My goodness, you're in a terrible hurry."

Nora didn't dare look behind her. If Haywood was in the corridor, and Lady Abercrombie saw her dashing away from him... Wait, how could that be bad?

Because this was London, and she was Lady Abercrombie. She would make it something bad.

Nora rubbed a hand over her own elbow where she'd crashed into Lady Abercrombie. It was a shame she hadn't knocked the other woman down. "Please excuse me."

She tried to walk more sedately to the drawing room, but her blood was rushing in her ears, and it felt as though she'd toppled out of the boat after all and was struggling to breach the surface of the water.

Lady Satterfield was waiting for her in the drawing room and was thankfully alone. When she saw Nora, a small crease formed between her brows. "Is something wrong? You look flushed."

Nora winced. She moved closer to the countess and spoke softly, "I'm afraid I took a wrong turn when I left the retiring room and ran into Lord Haywood."

Lady Satterfield's expression deepened to a frown. "I see. Did anything happen?" She also kept her voice low.

Oh no, did Lady Satterfield think Nora would've repeated the same mistake again?

The countess's face softened. "Not *that*, dear. I meant, did he make any untoward advances?"

"Only verbally. I instructed him never to speak to me again."

Lady Satterfield laughed, which put Nora at ease. "Well done. I wish I could've seen it." She linked her arm through Nora's, and they left the house. "On that note, did anyone see you?"

"Not with him, but I ran into Lady Abercrombie on my way back. If she saw Lord Haywood…" Nora couldn't bring herself to verbalize her fear.

Lady Satterfield patted Nora's forearm. "Do not worry yourself about it. She saw nothing. Anything she says will be innuendo."

"But that's enough to ruin someone, isn't it?"

"It can be…damaging, but I'll ensure that it isn't."

Nora sent her a disbelieving look as they walked back down to the grass. "How will you manage that miracle?"

The countess smiled. "Leave that to me, my dear. One doesn't spend three decades amongst the ton without learning how to survive and how to protect those we care about."

Nora's heart swelled. For a brief moment, it almost felt as though she had a mother again. And that sentiment was enough to drive away the disquiet Haywood had left her with.

For now.

TITUS STALKED INTO his office, intent on the whisky decanter. He was glad for the abbreviated session in the House of Lords tonight. He loosened his cravat as he arrived at the sideboard. As he poured his whisky, he worked to shove the evening's business from his mind—he was weary of discussing the Luddites.

Instead, he preferred to focus on the pleasant afternoon he'd spent at Brexham Hall. He'd enjoyed his brief walk with Nora more than he ought to admit.

He wished he'd skipped the infernal meeting and stayed to take her out in one of the boats. Instead, she'd likely gone with Dawson, a gentleman Titus didn't even know but longed to remove from her presence.

Really? He wanted to deny her the very thing she was trying to gain? She wanted a husband. She deserved a husband. Or at least happiness. And if a husband would afford that, then that was what she deserved.

"Your Grace?" Abbott, the butler who'd overseen this town house in Titus's father's time, stood at the threshold. "There is a letter from Lady Satterfield on your desk. It arrived while you were out."

Titus took a drink of whisky as he went and located the note from his stepmother. He set the glass down to open the paper. Immediately, a cold sweat dappled the back of his neck.

Kendal,
I am concerned that a rumor that has started about Miss Lockhart will spread. She was seen leaving a private rendezvous with Lord Haywood this afternoon. It was a chance meeting and one that no one witnessed, but the woman who saw her immediately afterward—that detestable Lady Abercrombie—seems intent on disparaging Nora. I'm going to do my best to quash any gossip, and would appreciate any help you can offer.
Lady S

Rage heated his blood and sent tremors through his hands. He crumpled the paper and dropped it on his desk. "Abbott," he barked.

"Yes, Your Grace?"

"Have my coach brought back around— I'm going to the club." He meant to find Haywood and ensure the knave never again came within fifty paces of Nora.

"Yes, Your Grace." Abbot didn't question

the sudden change of Titus's evening plans, which was a bit surprising. Titus didn't remember the last time he'd done anything spontaneously.

But this was necessary. He picked up his whisky and tossed it down his throat in its entirety. The liquor warmed his belly, stoking the anger that the lecherous Haywood had provoked.

A scant twenty minutes later, Titus strode into Brooks's and immediately walked into the subscription room, where a good number of London's gentlemen would be gambling and drinking. He scanned the tables for Haywood and located him seated near the corner, playing whist.

He strode to his former crony with purpose, aware that dozens of pairs of eyes followed him. When he arrived at the table, the occupants looked up at him in concert, but he noted this from the periphery of his vision—his primary focus was on the reprobate who'd dared insult Miss Lockhart a second time. "Stand up, Haywood." He kept his voice low and didn't give a whit that it carried a dark menace. In fact, he *liked* that.

Haywood's eyes widened, and he briefly touched his chest, looking mildly affronted. "I'm in the middle of a hand."

"I wouldn't care if you were in the middle

of using the privy. *Stand up.*"

Haywood's brow furrowed. "Really, Kendal, I must ask that you wait."

"It's quite all right," said the gentleman to Haywood's left. "We'll pause the game."

Haywood looked at his tablemates. "If you're certain you don't mind."

Titus's patience withered until it was nearly gone. He was about to physically drag the man out of his chair when he finally stood.

"Come." Titus bit out the command and gestured for Haywood to follow him. He led the scoundrel to his private chamber.

"What the devil is going on?" Haywood asked as they mounted the stairs. "You haven't spoken to me in nearly a decade, and now you interrupt a perfectly smashing game of whist. I hope you haven't upset my streak."

Titus waited to answer until they were inside his private room. A footman opened the door and closed it behind Haywood. It took everything Titus had not to *smash* his fist into the man's ruddy face.

"I haven't spoken to you in a decade because I haven't had reason to. Now, however, I have a reason, and you will heed every word I say. You are going to deny that you saw Miss Lockhart today."

Haywood appeared utterly nonplussed. "I

already said that I did."

Titus's right hand curled into a fist. How he ached to hit the man. "Say you were mistaken. Furthermore, you are not to speak to Miss Lockhart again. You are not to speak *of* Miss Lockhart. You are not to come within fifty paces of Miss Lockhart. In fact, you are not to *look* at Miss Lockhart. Do I make myself clear?"

With each directive, Haywood's mouth had opened a little further until his jaw had gone completely slack. He stood like that, gaping at Titus for a moment. He closed his mouth and did the damnedest—no, the *stupidest* thing. He *laughed*. "I beg your pardon? Is this some sort of joke?"

Titus took a step toward him. "*You* are the only joke in this room."

Haywood sobered. "Now, there's no call to be rude. Why do you care if I speak to Miss Lockhart?"

"Because you ruined her chances at a decent, happy life once, and I won't allow you to do it again."

"Who are you? Her father?" He laughed again, but without humor this time. "This is rich. You used to be the worst rake in town."

"*Used* to be. We've matured past that, haven't we, Haywood?" He took another step toward him. "Or are you still behaving like a lad who can't keep his cock in his breeches?"

Haywood's eyes narrowed. "You go too far."

Another step forward. "I'm not sure I've gone far enough. If you so much as *think* of Miss Lockhart, let alone approach her, you will be sorry."

Something lit in Haywood's gaze—an acknowledgment of Titus's anger, perhaps. "I have no reason to speak with her again anyhow. She propositioned me—a married man." He shook his head. "She's every bit the trollop she was all those years ago."

Titus didn't think. He just acted. His fist connected with Haywood's half smirk, sending the degenerate's head snapping backward.

"Christ!" Haywood's hand came up against his mouth as his tongue darted out to catch the blood from his split lip.

"I believe I told you not to speak of her, and yet you did. Do it again, and you'll be looking for a second."

This seemed to finally sink into Haywood's pea-sized brain. He blanched as he licked another drop of blood from his lip. He nodded slowly, his eyes failing to meet Titus's.

Titus moved past him, catching his shoulder against Haywood's bicep and knocking him off-balance. He opened the door and addressed the footman in the corridor. "Please have this rubbish removed from my chamber."

Titus didn't look back as he made his way downstairs. Energy still thrummed through him as if he'd raced his horse across his estate at a breakneck pace, but there was satisfaction too. And that was a damn sight better than the outrage he'd felt earlier.

When he reached the subscription room, he was aware of the buzz dying more quickly than usual, of the stares that seemed to burn straight through his coat. He'd created a bit of a sensation by directly approaching Haywood and taking him upstairs, and that rankled. He could only imagine what they would say when they learned he'd hit Haywood. But Haywood wouldn't tell them that. He was vain and self-important enough to fabricate a story to explain his split lip. Still, people would draw their own conclusions.

Titus shrugged the irritation away. People would *always* draw their own conclusions. And there was nothing he could do about it, save intimidate them, which he was not above doing. Instead of keeping his attention forward and ignoring everyone as he typically did, he sent a few well-directed stares, silently communicating that they should all mind their own business. Would they? How much influence did the Forbidden Duke really carry?

He didn't really give a damn what any of them thought. He did, however, care what they thought of Nora. She hadn't deserved what had happened to her nine years ago, and she sure as hell didn't deserve it now. She especially didn't deserve Haywood causing her yet more heartache.

At least that would stop. Titus was certain he'd successfully prevented Haywood from bothering her again. He'd pen a note to his stepmother as soon as he returned home and assure her of that fact.

Then he ought to visit his mistress. He still hadn't been to see her since that first night. He'd much rather visit Nora and ensure she was all right after her encounter with Haywood, but he wouldn't do that either. No, he'd do what he'd done every night the past week—he'd go home alone and dream of an auburn-haired beauty with enchanting tawny eyes.

He had to accept that he was far more interested in Nora than he ought to be. This changed nothing, however. He wasn't looking for a wife, and if he were, she would never want him once she learned the truth about the past. It was past time he quashed his inconvenient attraction.

Chapter Eight
⊹ɛ·꒱⊹

WHEN NORA CAME down to dinner the following evening, she stopped short in the doorway. Kendal stood near the table, talking to Lord Satterfield. He looked terribly handsome, dressed in an impeccable dark blue coat and pantaloons that had to be the absolute latest in the style of men's garments. They hugged his thighs, presenting an exceptional portrait of a virile gentleman.

"Kendal, you've come for dinner!" Lady Satterfield's exclamation came from just behind Nora.

Both men turned to look at the doorway, and Nora fought to keep a blush from staining her cheeks. They could have no idea that she'd been standing there gaping at Kendal. Lady Satterfield, on the other hand, might very well have caught her in the act.

Nora moved into the dining room along with Lady Satterfield, who went to her stepson. Kendal bussed her cheek in greeting. "I hope it's no trouble that I've come."

"Never. I see your place has already been set," she said. "Let us sit. Harley looks ready to serve."

Satterfield always sat at the head, with his wife at his right and Nora on his left. Tonight there were two seats on the left, which meant she'd be sitting next to Kendal.

While Satterfield held his wife's chair, Kendal performed the same service for Nora.

"Thank you," she murmured, feeling unaccountably nervous.

The first course, including soup, boiled beef, and carrots was served, and wine was poured. Nora had been overwhelmed by the wealth of food since her arrival at the Satterfields, but was beginning to grow accustomed to it. It wasn't that she and her father had gone hungry, but they'd led a very simple life.

"The weather has been exceptional," Satterfield said. "Did you ride today, Kendal?"

"I did." He looked at Nora. "Do you ride?"

"Not well. My cousins—they sponsored my first Seasons—introduced me to it, but I never mastered the sport, I'm afraid."

"We shall have to rectify that," Lady

Satterfield said. "I can picture you in a cunning riding hat. We shall have to shop for a habit."

Kendal chuckled as he flashed his stepmother a look. "And what of the horse? She'll need something to ride."

"We have a horse." She looked at her husband. "Don't we, dear?"

"Not one that is suitable for Nora. However, I'm certain Kendal has an appropriate mount." He sent a questioning look at the duke.

Before Kendal could respond, Lady Satterfield interjected. "I just remembered that Mrs. Gilchrist invited us to ride at their house outside town." She looked at Nora. "Would you feel comfortable doing that?"

Nora had met Mrs. Gilchrist and her son Mr. Barnaby Gilchrist yesterday at the picnic. She'd taken a walk with Mr. Gilchrist, and he'd talked mostly of horses. And fish. She'd enjoyed her time with Mr. Dawson more. But then neither could compare to Kendal.

She stole a quick glance in his direction. His dark hair brushed the top of the white collar at the back of his head. The contrast was striking, especially when compared with the warm bronze of his skin. He was clean-shaven, but she could detect the dark shadow beginning to creep over his jaw.

She looked away quickly, lest he catch her.

"Nora?"

Lady Satterfield's query reminded her that she'd forgotten to answer. "I think I'd prefer to wait to ride in public until I've mastered at least a few practice walks."

"Kendal, do let us know when you can take her for a ride," Lady Satterfield said.

The duke looked at Nora, and the impact of his gaze curled her toes. Goodness, she was as fervent as she'd been in her youth. Had she learned nothing? Resolved to ignore her attraction to the duke, she focused on her meal and tried to think of Mr. Dawson, who likely wouldn't care if she could ride or not.

"Kendal, how are your stables at Lakemoor?" Satterfield asked. "We didn't venture up for a visit this past fall. I shall make it a priority this year. You put on quite a hunt."

Nora peeked over at him. Did he host a hunting party? She was surprised, given his reputation. She didn't think he socialized at all.

"It's a small affair, if you recall."

"Yes, but I like that. So many hunting parties have little to do with hunting." Satterfield chuckled. "Or so it seems."

"That's because Kendal only invites local gentlemen and you, my dear," Lady

Satterfield said. "It isn't a proper house party at all." She looked at her stepson with slightly pursed lips but said nothing more.

"It *isn't* a house party." Kendal's tone was light, but there was a thread of steel.

Nora had the sense that Lady Satterfield wasn't pleased with Kendal's lack of social activity.

Lady Satterfield sighed. "Yes, yes, I know." She sipped her wine, then offered her stepson a warm smile. "Whatever makes you happy, dear."

Was that what made him happy? Keeping to himself? Did he prefer isolation? Having endured nine years of that, Nora suppressed a shudder. While she'd found Society challenging, she couldn't imagine going back to a life of seclusion and hoped she wouldn't have to.

The conversation turned to a variety of topics—from Kendal's work in the House of Lords to Nora's family to the theater. It was, overall, one of the most pleasant evenings Nora had spent, and by the end of the last course, she'd actually relaxed in the duke's presence. Maybe he wasn't so forbidden after all. At least not to his close family—not that she believed she was one of them, but for now, she could perhaps enjoy this familiarity.

"It's a lovely evening," Lady Satterfield

said as she placed her napkin on the table. "Kendal, why don't you take Nora for a walk around the garden?"

Nora's heartbeat sped. There went the comfort she'd only just found.

But why? It was a walk, nothing more, through a very small walled garden. And maybe he didn't even want to go.

"Certainly." Kendal stood and helped Nora from her chair.

Apparently, he did want to go. Or he was merely being polite.

Lord Satterfield assisted Lady Satterfield. "I'm off to my club for a bit." He pressed a kiss to his wife's cheek.

She leaned close with a warm smile before looking toward Nora and Kendal. "And I'll just be up in my sitting room answering some correspondence. I don't think I need to chaperone you for such a short jaunt."

They all went their separate ways—Lord and Lady Satterfield exiting the dining room into the main hallway and Kendal and Nora to the rear sitting room, which functioned as a library and general gathering space for the family. Kendal offered Nora his arm and led her into the cozy room in which she'd spent several evenings reading from the Satterfields' excellent collection of books.

The library was not a small chamber; however, it seemed somehow smaller tonight. Kendal's presence seemed to invade every nook and inhabit every cranny, and Nora was nearly overcome with awareness. And nervousness.

She rushed to say something to put herself at ease. "I quite enjoy the Satterfields' library."

He paused, pivoting toward the bookcases that marched along one wall. "Do you? What are your favorites?"

Nora wondered what he'd think of her tastes, which ran the gamut from romantic novels to gothic tales to poetry to suspenseful narratives. "I have many. I'm afraid it's difficult to choose."

"What's the last one you read, then?"

She hesitated, but only briefly. "A romantic novel by Sarah Wilkinson." Presumably, he'd find her tastes lacking.

"I've read all of her books."

Nora looked up at him in surprise. "*You read Sarah Wilkinson?*"

He gave her a sly look. "Perhaps you noticed that Lady Satterfield owns every title. She's always had a penchant for such stories, and, in my youth, I read everything I could get my hands on. *Everything.*"

Nora pressed her fingers to her mouth and giggled. "Do you like romantic novels?"

"I don't *dislike* them. If I'm in a particular mood, I've been known to read three or four in a week."

Her giggles turned to outright laughter. "The Forbidden Duke reads tawdry romances? What would the ton say?"

"I don't give a damn what anyone says, but I suppose that would cause a stir."

How lovely it must be not to care—not to *have* to care—what others said about you. "Everything you do causes a stir," she said, her laughter dying down. "The novels would make you seem more human, however." She inwardly winced at how awful that sounded. "Oh dear, please forgive me. I didn't mean to infer you aren't human."

He took her hand and tucked her fingers beneath his coat, guiding her palm flat against his waistcoat directly over his heart. "You can feel that I am."

Nora's breath caught. She looked up at him, her gaze locking with his. "I never doubted it."

He let go of her hand, and she slowly, reluctantly let it fall to her side. Frissons of excitement danced up her arms and spread, awakening her senses.

"You are correct, however, that others perhaps view me differently," he said. "I don't allow them the opportunity to be this close."

Yet he was permitting her. Again, she considered that he did so only because she was his stepmother's ward. But because she was curious and impetuous, she asked, "Why am I different?" Immediately she wanted to take it back. She *wasn't* different, of course. She was simply *here.* "Please forget I asked. You are too kind to pay attention to me and support my cause."

His lips twisted into a slight frown. "I'm not doing this out of kindness."

She wasn't precisely certain what "this" meant, but she wasn't going to ask for clarification. "Then why are you doing it?"

"I don't know." He fingered a wisp of hair that grazed her ear. It was a singular moment, as if time ceased to exist between them. But it was fleeting too. He quickly retreated from her, turning his back as he went toward the fireplace. "I didn't mean to overstep."

He turned once he was a safe distance from her. "I wanted to ask if you were all right after Haywood insulted you at the picnic." His tone was crisp, almost businesslike, but it didn't calm the sudden tumult of anxiety that spilled through her.

She'd so hoped her encounter with Haywood would go unnoticed, but it seemed scandal might plague her again. "What did you hear?"

"I don't listen to gossip. My stepmother informed me of his unwanted attention toward you." His brows pitched low for a brief moment. "I've ensured he won't bother you again."

She couldn't begin to imagine what that meant. "What did you do?"

He glanced away from her and shrugged. "He knows he's not to speak with you or even speak *of* you. Not only do I not listen to gossip, I don't tolerate it concerning people I care about."

Nora froze. He *cared* about her? The rush of panic she'd felt at being at the heart of another scandal faded and was replaced with a warmth she couldn't quite name. "I still don't know what I did to gain your family's support. I…thank you."

"Why do you think you have to have done something?" His dark brows drew together, and while he didn't look exactly fierce, he possessed an intensity that could very well be intimidating. "Are you that unused to kindness?"

Yes, in fact, but she couldn't bring herself to admit such a shameful truth. She laughed, but it held a ring of discomfort. "You must agree that it's a bit extraordinary for a prominent family—a duke's family—

to take in a young woman like me."

"Like you," he repeated. It wasn't a question, but he said it in such a way he seemed to want to know what she meant. Surely he knew of her background. They hadn't spoken directly of it, but of course he knew.

She wanted to be certain. She looked him straight in the eye. "A woman who has been ruined by scandal."

He slowly arched his brow. "You deserve to be here. You deserve to find happiness—everyone does."

A kind and thoughtful Untouchable who seemed to find her interesting... She couldn't tear her gaze away from his potent stare. "What about you, Your Grace? Are you happy?"

"I'm not *un*happy."

She resisted the urge to smile. "That's not exactly a resounding proclamation of joy."

"I am quite happy at Lakemoor. I enjoy working with my tenants. I enjoy my horses."

"And reading tawdry romance novels. Please don't leave out the most interesting thing about you."

A laugh erupted from his chest, and Nora gave in to her grin. "Yes, let's not leave that out." He walked across the room toward her, coming as close as he'd been before.

"Shall we resume our walk?"

He took her hand and curled it around his forearm. His heat, his scent, his proximity filled her senses. She clasped him more tightly with the need to anchor herself.

The familiarity she'd believed to have sprung up between them at dinner and over the course of their other encounters suddenly transformed into something else—intimacy. And with it came a hunger for this man who said she deserved to be happy, who danced with her, and who'd come to her rescue with Haywood. She longed to stroke her fingers along the firm line of his jaw, perhaps feel the hairs sprouting there now at the end of the day. Would they be prickly or soft? Tantalizing or abrasive? Tantalizing, she was certain.

More than that, she wondered what his lips would feel like on hers. The solitary kiss she'd experienced nine years ago hadn't been pleasant, even before the scandal had broken. She hadn't been in a hurry to try it again, not that she'd had the chance. But now, standing here so close to Kendal, she couldn't help but think his kiss would be different. His kiss would be everything she'd dreamed of and more.

She reminded herself that she couldn't kiss him, and that she probably shouldn't even be alone with him. This was precisely what had landed her in trouble in the first place. Oh, but if she could kiss him without anyone finding out...

Walking with him in the garden was perhaps a foolish idea, but Nora still couldn't bring herself to say no.

Chapter Nine
❧❦❧

TITUS GUIDED HER out onto the terrace, then down the pair of steps into his stepmother's garden. "It might be small, but Lady Satterfield prides herself on the roses in particular. You should see the gardens at their country home."

He was fairly certain his attempt at small talk was pathetic in the extreme, but his brain was having a difficult time outpacing his body at present. The touch of Nora's hand on his arm, the sensuous curl of her lips as she spoke to him, the provocative slant of her tawny eyes—all of it triggered an exquisite need.

Walking with her in the garden was a bloody terrible idea. But he was doing it anyway.

He steered her toward the roses he'd mentioned. They weren't blooming yet, but in a few weeks, they'd be a riot of color and a buffet of gorgeous scents.

She inclined her head toward the neat row of shrubs. "We have roses back in St. Ives. Tending to them was one of my favorite summertime activities."

He envisioned her alone in the country, clipping at rosebushes, perhaps pricking her fingers on their nasty thorns. Somehow that seemed a metaphor for Society— beautiful but treacherous. "Will you miss that? I'm sure my stepmother wouldn't mind if you wanted to tinker with these."

She smiled. "Thank you, but I think she will have me too busy with other things. She's quite committed to ensuring I have a Season to remember."

Complete with a husband. He barely managed not to scowl.

They walked for a moment in silence. He should leave. He'd only come to dinner because he enjoyed dining with his stepparents. Except now, that dinner came with a beguiling woman who occupied far too many of his thoughts. A woman he'd pledged to avoid but couldn't seem to.

She tipped her head toward him. "I hope you won't find me impudent, but I wonder if I could ask how you ended up with the nickname of the Forbidden Duke."

He stopped and pivoted toward her.

She winced and withdrew her hand from his arm. "I'm sorry. Lady Satterfield has indicated you're a man who values his privacy. Forget that I asked."

"It's not as if I cultivated the name," he

said. "At least not on purpose. I can't say I dislike it either. People cut me a wide swath, which means I don't have to suffer banality. For that, I am quite relieved."

She laughed. "My goodness. I can't decide if you're a snob or just intensely aloof." She slapped her hand over her mouth, her beautiful eyes widening.

He laughed with her, delighting in her honesty even while acknowledging that if anyone else had said that to him, he'd give them the cut direct. "Probably a bit of both."

Her eyes lit with mirth. "So you enjoy being forbidden?"

"I *enjoy* being left alone. If not for my responsibilities in the House of Lords, I would hardly come to London."

She sobered. "I see. I am just the opposite, I'm afraid. I've been alone for so long that I'm quite eager to be among people."

Her tone was matter-of-fact, but there was something else lurking in the depths of her eyes—an uncertainty or perhaps a sadness. Whatever it was, he wanted to banish it. He moved closer to her, drawn like a raindrop to the earth. His blood was roaring in his ears in a thoroughly primal fashion.

Again, he thought that he shouldn't be

here with her. This moment could be a scandal in the making.

Only if there was a witness, his mind whispered.

"I enjoy talking with you," he said. "It's a crime that you were alone for so long."

Her lashes fluttered. "I enjoy talking with you too." Her voice was low, unintentionally seductive.

He desperately wanted to touch her, determine for himself if her flesh was as soft and warm as he imagined. So he did.

His fingers grazed her jaw. She sucked in a breath, and the sound evoked an even greater physical response, sending his body into complete abandon.

"We should return to the house." Her words were barely audible, scarcely more than a breath.

Yes, they should, but he hated the ton's stupid rules. Right now, he wanted to rebel against them. "We should. Only..." He wanted to kiss her. So badly. But he couldn't. Not because of the rules, but because of what she'd already been through nine years ago.

He edged backward and was shocked when she placed her hand on his lapel. Her touch was light, hesitant.

"Would you...kiss me?" she asked softly. "I've only ever been kissed that one time, and it was awful." She blinked rapidly and snatched her hand away. "Never mind. I'm far too brazen." Her face colored, and he could practically feel her embarrassment.

He didn't want her to be embarrassed. Nor did he want to deny her request. "You are not. It's a sin that you haven't been kissed properly."

He stepped closer and lowered his head. He went slowly in case she changed her mind, but thankfully she did not. When his lips met hers, a dark pulse of desire swelled through him. He worked to keep a rein on himself. It would be so easy to get lost in her kiss.

Her hands came back against his chest, but more firmly this time. Her lips pressed into his, evidencing her participation. But then hadn't she asked him to?

Yes, and he was going to make it good for her.

He tilted his head and lifted his lips briefly before kissing her again. He danced his mouth against hers, keeping himself in check while she acclimated herself to his touch. When her hands crept up to his shoulders, he took it as a sign to go further.

He put his arms around her and pulled her more snugly against him and parted his mouth against hers. Her fingers dug into his shoulders, and he worried she would push him away.

Please, not yet.

This kiss was too honest, too beautiful, and he wasn't ready for it to end. Not until he'd shown her a proper kiss.

He licked along the crease of her mouth, and she opened, perhaps in surprise. When he plunged his tongue inside, her grip became even tighter. Still, she didn't pull back or shove at him. Instead, she tipped her head to the side, and it was all the invitation he needed.

He brought her flush against him, heedless of any sense of propriety. He stroked along her spine as he plundered her mouth. Her tongue met his, softly at first, but then more purposefully. He wasn't sure at what precise moment this had progressed from a demonstration to a thoroughly impulsive act, but it had crossed that line, and Titus was in real danger of losing control.

With supreme effort, he pulled his mouth from hers and stepped back. "My deepest apologies, Miss Lockhart."

Forget Haywood; Titus was the one who deserved a thorough thrashing. And yet, he couldn't regret kissing her, nor could he stop himself from wanting to do it again.

But he wouldn't.

She lifted her other hand to her mouth.

Her eyes were wary, but something else flickered there—a spark of heat in the tawny depths. "Thank you. That was…quite different from last time."

He laughed—he couldn't help himself. "I am glad to have obliged you. But we can't do that again."

She dropped her hand to her side. "No, I suppose we can't." The look she gave him next brought his cock to full arousal. Her scalding gaze dipped down his frame and then back up to his eyes. "Pity."

"Miss Lockhart, if you don't go back inside right now, my self-restraint will be in shreds."

Her eyes widened briefly just before she spun on her heel and hastened through the garden on her way back to the house. She didn't spare him a backward glance before disappearing inside.

He exhaled, realizing he'd been holding his breath while she fled. Damn, he was a lecherous beast.

Hadn't he threatened Haywood for doing precisely what he'd just done? Perhaps not *precisely*, but the end result would be the same—the ruination of a lady who deserved far better. And she was so close to the life she ought to have had.

A phantom voice in his head said he could give her that life if *he* married her. *No,* he didn't want a wife. A wife was a nuisance, something he should probably have but didn't particularly want or need, and even if he did, it wouldn't be her. Once she learned the truth about his past, the role he'd played in her downfall, she would—rightfully—despise him. What sort of marriage would that be?

No, she deserved someone honorable, someone like Dawson, who clearly wanted a wife. He would treat her well, provide her with a comfortable life, and her past would be forgotten.

A small part of Titus hoped she wouldn't forget their kiss. He knew he wouldn't.

◆·ᏋᎶ·◆

THE FOLLOWING EVENING, Nora and Lady Satterfield were on their way to one of the largest balls of the Season. Hosted by the Duke and Duchess of Colne, it was bound to be a crush from everything Nora had heard. And she'd heard plenty that afternoon at the park.

Lady Satterfield looked through the window and craned her neck to try to see down the street. "My goodness, we're backed up already. This is going to be quite a throng." She looked at Nora with an animated expression. "I do hope Satterfield can find us."

Lord Satterfield would be joining them later after starting the evening at his club.

With a sparkle in her eye, the countess turned her attention to Nora. "Tell me, who do you most hope to dance with tonight?"

Kendal.

But Nora didn't say that. He wouldn't be here in any case. "I expect I'll dance with Mr. Dawson, and perhaps Lord Markham or Mr. Gilchrist."

"Mr. Dawson seems taken with you. Do you feel the same?"

He was charming and witty and reasonably attractive. But he was no Kendal, whom she couldn't stop thinking of since last night's kiss. "He's quite pleasant."

Lady Satterfield brushed at her skirt. "I see. Well, that is not a glowing declaration."

"I didn't mean to disparage him at all. I do like him."

"But do you like him enough to accept a proposal should he offer for you? It's one thing to like a gentleman, and quite another to agree to spend your life with him. For some women, that sentiment is enough. For others, they might prefer to marry for love or…passion." She gave Nora a meaningful look.

Yes, passion. Like the kiss she'd shared with Kendal last night. No matter how pleasant she found Mr. Dawson, she doubted he could make her feel like that. Furthermore, she wasn't sure she wanted to find out.

"Anyway, you needn't settle on Mr. Dawson—or anyone else for that matter—any time soon. Your popularity is only increasing, and I expect you will have several suitors clamoring for your attention." She smiled widely as she leaned forward and gave Nora's knee a quick pat.

"Thank you," Nora said, grateful for any reprieve. Everything was moving so quickly. She'd gone from needing a job to provide for her future to being the toast of the ton.

She was having a hard time deciding what to wear. Selecting a potential bridegroom seemed a dizzying task.

Indeed, she found herself missing her quiet life in St. Ives—her roses and her books. Visits with her sister. She wrote to Jo nearly every day and eagerly awaited her sister's replies, which came at the same pace. Jo was happy for Nora's second chance, while at the same time astounded, like Nora, that she'd been given such a boon. Her father, on the other hand, had written only once—to say that he was now settled with his sister and brother-in-law. Nora felt sad to think that there was now nothing for her to go home to. In fact, she didn't really have a home, unless she considered the Satterfields', and she supposed she must.

"So what sort of marriage do you think you'd prefer?" Lady Satterfield asked. "I've been fortunate enough to fall in love twice. I admit I'd like to see the same happen for you." She spoke with warmth and sincerity, and Nora was nearly overcome with gratitude and appreciation. In many ways, Lady Satterfield had become a surrogate mother, and, honestly, she was the best thing about all the abrupt changes in Nora's life. The memory of Kendal's kiss rose in her mind. Perhaps not the *best* thing…

"Love would be nice," Nora said. "However, I have no illusions at my age. I should be quite happy to find companionship and mutual admiration."

"Don't settle for something you don't want. The right man is out there. I'm certain of it." Lady Satterfield looked out the window again. "Ah, we've finally arrived."

The footman opened the door and helped the countess step down from the carriage. The night was cool but dry.

Nora took the footman's proffered hand

and stepped from the carriage. Then she followed Lady Satterfield to the door of the massive town house. Situated in the heart of Upper Grosvenor Street, the Colnes' address was exceedingly fashionable. It was a place Nora could never have hoped to visit during her prior Seasons. Now, however, she seemed to have infiltrated the uppermost circle and could rub shoulders with the Untouchables. She felt like an utter fraud.

As they made their way inside and through the receiving line, Nora allowed her mind to wander. She paid just enough attention to the proceedings so as not to make a fool of herself, while indulging the fantasies taking root in her brain. She thought of a future where she didn't have to choose a husband at all, but could instead be independent and carefree. In that dream world, she'd kiss whomever she wanted with impunity.

"Miss Lockhart, you are a vision!" Mr. Dawson greeted her with a grin, his brown eyes lighting with appreciation. "I do hope I'm the first to claim a dance this evening."

"Indeed you are."

"Excellent, I shall find you when the set begins." He gave her a brief bow before taking himself off.

Over the course of the next quarter hour,

Nora collected enough dance invitations to last her the entire evening. She ought to feel excited. After all, this was what she'd wanted, wasn't it?

Except now that she had it, she wasn't at all sure she was satisfied. It suddenly felt as though she'd taken her life of the past nine years for granted.

She danced with Mr. Dawson and tried to imagine a marriage with him. The *passion* Lady Satterfield had mentioned was nonexistent. But at the same time, he would make a perfectly acceptable husband.

That sounded so dull.

She danced with two more gentlemen before the supper break. When the music stopped, her partner led her from the dance floor, apologizing that he wasn't going to stay for supper. Nora was suddenly quite glad, because there, standing beside Lady Satterfield, was the last person she expected to see tonight—the Forbidden Duke.

Kendal watched her approach, his green eyes dark and seductive, almost beckoning her. She felt a pull to walk directly to him, the memory of his lips on hers propelling her forward.

"Good evening, Miss Lockhart." His voice was deep and captivating.

She offered him a curtsey. "Good evening, Your Grace. It's a pleasure to see you here." She didn't intentionally infuse the comment with any sort of question, but dearly wanted to ask why he'd come. His attendance was bound to cause a stir.

The edge of his mouth ticked up. It wasn't a smile, but she recognized it as him understanding her unasked query, particularly because his eyes seemed to glow with a suppressed emotion. She had the sense he was amused by this situation, and she longed to ask why.

"I was hoping to claim the next dance."

Oh dear. Disappointment curled through her. Her popularity had never been more of a nuisance. "I am, unfortunately, already committed, Your Grace."

The look in his eyes dampened. "Well then, I shall have to settle for a promenade."

"Yes, after supper," Lady Satterfield said.

Nora had all but forgotten her presence. In fact, she'd all but forgotten that they were at a ball. It had seemed that just she and Kendal existed. How absurdly delightful.

Lord Satterfield joined them. "Kendal, this is a shock. Are you trying to set the ton on its ear?" He grinned at his stepson before turning to his wife. "Shall we go in to supper?"

"Indeed." Kendal presented his arm to

Nora, and they preceded the Satterfields to the dining room, where a lavish table was set. Nora had never seen such a display. The sheer quantity of dishes, silver, and glasses was enough to make her head swim.

She tipped her head toward Kendal. "What a staggering amount of crockery."

She kept her voice low, preferring their conversation to be as private as possible. She could feel the eyes of the room staring at them, could hear the questions and comments the guests were striving to keep quiet. She preferred to pretend that she and Kendal were alone in the garden at the Satterfields'. Or anywhere else, really.

He guided her to a chair next to Lady Satterfield. "I can't imagine supporting an event of this size. My stepmother's annual ball is quite daunting enough." He situated Nora in the chair, and then his touch was gone, leaving her cold.

Lady Satterfield looked at Nora and then her stepson. "It isn't so different. Of course, I don't have the space or retainers to carry off a ball of this proportion. But if I did, I would." She smiled, her eyes sparkling. "Nora, when you are wed, you may find yourself the hostess of a ball like this."

Nora had dreamed of such a thing in the early years following her ruin, but had never imagined it would come true. Even now, sitting amongst the ton's most elite—the Untouchables—and enjoying a level of acceptance she'd never imagined, she couldn't quite believe it was possible. Furthermore, now that it was, she wasn't at all certain that was what she wanted.

Kendal indicated the footman should pour him some claret. He turned to Nora. "Claret or Madeira?"

She looked at the footman. "Madeira, please."

A woman seated on the other side of Kendal spoke. "Kendal, it is such a boon to find you here this evening. You seem to be quite the man about town this Season."

Nora hadn't ever seen him converse with people. On the occasions she'd seen him publicly—at Lady Satterfield's ball and the picnic—he'd spoken only with his stepparents and Nora. She waited to see what he would do.

He turned his head toward the woman, and Nora would've traded her pin money to see his expression. She strained to hear what he would say.

"Yes."

The single word seemed to convey a wealth of meaning, the most important of which was, *Don't speak to me again.*

Or so it seemed.

He turned his head toward Nora. "Have you enjoyed the ball?"

"Yes, thank you." She darted a look across the table and saw that people, as expected, were watching them. She did her best to ignore them and wondered how Kendal did it. He seemed utterly immune to those around him. "How do you do it?" she whispered.

"What?" It wasn't quite a whisper, but the word was soft, and the bass tone made her shiver.

"Shut them all out," she said.

"Ah. That, I think, is a conversation for another time." He barely smiled. "But I promise we shall have it."

Lady Satterfield took over the bulk of the conversation while they ate supper. As the meal drew to a close, she peered around Nora. "Kendal, will you be staying?"

He shook his head. "I've been here long enough, don't you think?" The elevation of his eyebrow lent a note of humor to his question.

His stepmother chuckled. "Indeed. It's a shame you can't dance with Nora, but I daresay she doesn't require your assistance any longer."

There it was. Nora had long suspected Kendal was only showing interest in her because Lady Satterfield had asked him to, and now she knew it was true. Why, then, had he kissed her? She dashed a glance at him, feeling suddenly unsettled.

Everyone began to stand from the table. Kendal helped Nora from her chair and led her from the dining room. Back in the ballroom, he kissed her hand. "It's been a pleasure, Miss Lockhart. Enjoy the rest of your evening."

"Thank you, Your Grace. I shall." But not nearly so much as the past hour. Until she'd begun to feel like an obligation. Or a favor the Forbidden Duke was doing for his beloved stepmother.

As she watched him retreat from the ballroom, a part of her protested. Perhaps his interest had started that way, but she didn't think she'd misunderstood his ardor when they'd kissed or the humor they'd shared in conversation or the promise he'd just made her at dinner. No, he didn't seem indifferent. But neither did that mean he wanted anything more than to help her on her way to success.

She danced with several more gentlemen, but with each one, she imagined green eyes and a seductive smile. By the time she climbed into the coach with Lady Satterfield, she was exhausted.

"How do people survive an entire Season of such entertainment?" Nora asked. She'd surely have to sleep the day away tomorrow, but likely wouldn't. She rose early in the country, and had not yet broken that habit.

The countess laughed. "You become used to it, but of course I don't go out like this every night. I wouldn't be able to manage. It was different when I was younger." She studied Nora. "You don't like it?"

Nora didn't want to hurt Lady Satterfield's feelings. She was, after all, providing Nora with an exceptional opportunity, and Nora didn't want to seem ungrateful. "It's not that... It's just different."

"You'll get used to it. Once you're wed, you can dictate your social calendar. Look at Kendal. He doesn't bother with any of it." She shook her head. "I'm astounded he came tonight. It will be the primary topic of conversation tomorrow. If it isn't already."

"You didn't know he was coming?" Nora asked.

"No, and I didn't ask him to. I told him we would be here, of course."

She hadn't asked him to come. Which meant he'd attended—sought her out—of his own accord. The unease she'd felt earlier dispelled, leaving a warm feeling of contentment in its wake.

Lady Satterfield tipped her head to the side. "You must think him very odd. I know some people do, but then others recall what he was like before—in his youth."

Nora leaned slightly forward, eager to know more. "And how was that?"

"He was careless, an utter rake, truth be told. Then his father died, and he became the duke. Kendal—that is, Titus—felt his responsibility quite heavily and worked hard to be the sort of man his father would have wanted him to be."

Nora was entranced. She longed to unravel the mysteries of the Forbidden Duke. "What sort of man was that?"

"Kendal—my husband, that is—was the smartest man I knew. He ran his estates impeccably and was always championing a cause or five in Parliament. He was a reformer." She smiled, her gaze looking into the distance as if she were overcome with memories. "He had very little time for nonsense, or what he considered nonsense anyway."

"What did he consider nonsense?"

Lady Satterfield's lips curved up. "Balls like this one, though he would've made an appearance for supper as Satterfield did."

Nora noted that Satterfield stayed longer than that before taking his leave. "Did he spend much time at his club?"

"In the same way that Titus does—keeping to his private room for the most part."

Titus. A strong name that recalled the Greek Titans, it fit him. Nora imagined him in solitude and was surprised to find the image enticing. But then any image with him made her stomach curl with anticipation. She tried to think of the younger Titus, the rake, and found it nearly impossible. "I can't imagine Kendal as a reckless youth."

"Yes, well, he was." Lady Satterfield shook her head gently. "He drove his father mad with his antics."

"What manner of antics?"

"He ran with a fast crowd—racing phaetons, gambling, everything you might expect. He cut quite a figure. I'm surprised you don't remember him from when you were out. That would have been about the same time."

Nora tried to recall him but couldn't. "I didn't move in the same circles." Indeed, her only foray into the upper echelon had been when Haywood had paid her attention, and look at how that had turned out.

"He wasn't Kendal of course then," Lady Satterfield said. "He was the Marquess of

Ravenglass."

That name sparked a hint of memory, but Nora still couldn't place him.

Lady Satterfield yawned as the coach stopped in front of their town house. "Goodness, but I am tired. We shall take a respite tomorrow. I need to summon my energy since I'm hosting a tea the following day."

Nora was delighted to have a day of relaxation. Even so, she felt restless just now. The name Ravenglass nagged at the back of her mind, but she simply didn't remember Kendal from her earlier Seasons. When she fell asleep that night, she thought of a rake named Ravenglass and couldn't imagine how he'd become the Forbidden Duke.

Chapter Ten
❧

TITUS WENT FROM the ball to his mistress's house. Isabelle was out—at the theatre, according to her footman—so he waited for her. But after pouring a glass of whisky, instead of making himself comfortable, he paced.

She made a grand entrance into the small sitting room adjoining her bedchamber. Dressed in a gown of sparkling ruby satin decorated with gold ribbon, she looked like a gleaming jewel meant to be appreciated. Preened over.

He couldn't help but contrast her to Nora. She'd worn a simple but elegant ball gown made of a rich amber that made her auburn hair seem redder and her tawny eyes more luminescent. Where Isabelle commanded attention, Nora quietly lured you into her orbit, and once there, you were sorely tempted to never leave.

But he *had* left. He'd possessed no other choice unless he wanted to give the ton even more fodder.

"Kendal," Isabelle purred. "What a

divine surprise." She set her fur-lined shawl on the settee. "Give me a few minutes to prepare before you come in." She started toward her bedchamber.

"Wait. I should like to…talk." He took the armchair near the fireplace, beside which sat his whisky on a side table. He took a drink and gestured for her to sit too.

She perched on the settee, her expression bemused. "All right." She tugged her gloves off and set them beside her. Then she reached up and unpinned the feather from her impressively dressed hair. "What are we to discuss?"

He shrugged. "The weather. Whatever you saw at the theatre. I care not."

"I see. You came here to talk but haven't a subject in mind." She placed the feather atop her gloves. "I hope you'll forgive my boldness—you've a terrible reputation for not suffering foolishness of any kind—but why ever did you employ me?"

He suppressed a scowl and took another drink of whisky. "No, I do not suffer fools."

She narrowed her eyes. "You specifically told me that you chose me because I am blessedly bereft of the guile my *sisters* typically wield. Would you also prefer I hold my tongue? If memory serves, you quite liked that appendage."

She was referring to the night he'd taken her into his employ. They'd come back here to her small town house, the one he was now paying for, and she'd given evidence to the skills she'd claimed to possess. She was, without debate, an excellent lover. And he hadn't touched her since.

"I've been busy." She hadn't asked why he hadn't partaken of her services, but for some reason, he felt the need to explain. Now who was being foolish?

Isabelle smoothed her beautifully manicured hand over her skirt. "Well, I'm delighted you're here now. I've been most anxious to deepen our acquaintance." The look she gave him was seductively direct and left absolutely no room for misunderstanding. She meant to take him into her bedchamber and do whatever he wanted.

Only he didn't want that. Not with her. He realized he'd met Nora the day after he'd taken Isabelle.

Isabelle watched him for a moment, her expression turning from one of enticement to confusion. She abruptly stood and went to the sideboard, where she poured herself a glass of whisky. "Do you need a refill?" she asked.

Titus looked at his nearly empty glass on the table. "Yes, thank you."

She sauntered toward him with the decanter and filled the glass. When she was back at the sideboard, she turned toward him, cradling her glass. She seemed to study him intently before taking a sip. "Something's wrong. You don't want me, I think. And yet you did. What happened? Did you meet someone else?"

He didn't hesitate before answering. "Yes."

She pursed her lips. "I see. As it happens, I had other interested gentlemen. I am certain I could find another protector. Tell me, who is the hussy so I can spill my Madeira on her when next we meet?"

He nearly laughed at the venom in her tone. Courtesans could be vicious in their pursuit of a protector. "No, it isn't like that. She's not…like you."

Her eyes widened briefly, and she walked back to the settee, where she sat down again. "When you hired me, you demanded absolute secrecy about our relationship, including anything we discussed. I took the vow that I gave you very seriously. Do you wish to talk about her?"

He supposed he did. He'd come here in the hope that he might frig Isabelle senseless, but he didn't want to. No, when he thought of the woman he wanted to make love to tonight, it wasn't his mistress.

He cleared his throat. "Her name is Nora. She has, ah, captured my attention."

"How lovely for her. She must be over the moon to have snagged a duke."

He frowned. "It isn't like that. She is my stepmother's ward."

Isabelle's mouth formed an O. "She's quite young, then?"

"No, she's actually not." He wasn't sure of her precise age, but thought she was probably twenty-seven or twenty-eight. "In fact, she's older than you."

Isabelle's elegant blond brows climbed. "Indeed? How on earth did she come to be your mother's ward?"

He took a long pull on his whisky. "The details do not signify. Suffice it to say there are…reasons I cannot pursue her."

"Bah. You're a duke. *The Forbidden Duke.* Perhaps the most untouchable peer in the realm. You can pursue anyone you damn well please."

Her use of the word untouchable made him think of Nora. With that one word, she'd perfectly captured the not-so-subtle hierarchy within the ton. It was a hierarchy he despised, for it allowed him and his ilk to do what Isabelle had just said—anything they damn well pleased. While at the same time, it prevented people such as Nora from doing what they wanted. And it wasn't just social position dictating their roles—it was, of course, their sex. In his youth, Titus had exploited all of it—his position, his masculinity, his power.

To Nora's detriment.

"I can't pursue *her*."

Isabelle sipped her whisky. "Can't or won't? I still maintain you can do whatever you please. Any woman would be thrilled to have your attention." Her gaze dipped to his groin. "Whether you had a title or not."

Her delicate innuendo wasn't lost on him, but it didn't apply in this case. He finished off his whisky with a long swallow and stood. "It was a mistake for me to come here."

She also stood, depositing her glass on the low table between them as she did so. "Where are you going?"

He hadn't thought that far. Part of him wanted to hunt down all the men who'd clogged Nora's dance card tonight and thrash them. Of course he wouldn't. Besides, he'd already drawn enough notice by going to that damned ball in the first place. Why had he done that? Because he'd wanted to see Nora. Needed to. After their kiss, he'd been utterly consumed with thoughts of her.

Isabelle came around the table and stood before him. She touched his chest, gingerly at first, then pressing her palm against his coat. "You could stay."

He put his hand over hers and gently guided it away from him. "Thank you, but no. I think you should take a new protector. I'll take care of you until you find one."

She pouted, but in a thoroughly attractive fashion, as if she'd perfected the expression through years of practice. "I would rather keep you."

"I'm afraid that is not an option. I am sorry." He moved away from her and walked to the doorway to the hall.

"I'm sorry too. She's a lucky woman."

He almost laughed. She'd been anything but. Until now. Now, she was cresting a wave that would see her settled in the life she'd always wanted. A life he wouldn't be a part of.

⋆⛬⋆

NORA COULDN'T SLEEP. She ought to be in the arms of Morpheus, but her brain simply wouldn't turn off. She kept replaying her time at the ball with Titus. And their kiss.

She crept downstairs to the library to find a book. Maybe that would help her relax.

The opposite happened as she opened

the door and froze. Titus was standing in front of the bookshelves, a glass of whisky dangling from his fingertips.

He looked at her standing on the threshold, and his eyes dipped over her. The perusal was slow, deliberate, intoxicating. "Good evening again, Miss Lockhart."

"What are you doing here?" she blurted and immediately damned her loose tongue for the thousandth time. "I'm sure it's none of my concern. I'll leave you to it." She turned, but felt the air shift. Then his hand was on her arm.

"Stay." He often spoke in single words, yet managed to color them with such inflection that they carried far more meaning. Or so her fanciful mind believed. He said, "Stay," but she heard warmth and something more—something beyond a simple invitation. Something akin to what she felt: need.

She tilted her head and looked down at where his fingers caressed the sleeve of her night robe. She realized she was barely garbed. This was beyond scandalous.

She turned toward him. "I should not."

He shrugged. "No one will know." He glanced down at the glass in his other hand. "Would you care for a drink?"

She looked up into his eyes. "That is

hardly appropriate."

"Nothing about this is, so why should we care?" He gently tugged her farther into the room and then left her briefly to close the door. No, there was absolutely nothing appropriate about any of this. She ought to leave, but she simply couldn't. She wanted this moment for herself. Certainly she'd earned it.

"Whisky?" she asked.

"Yes." He went to the sideboard. "Is that all right, or would you prefer sherry?"

Sherry was the more feminine choice, but she'd sampled whisky with her father a time or two. "I should say sherry, but I believe I'll take whisky."

He chuckled. She loved that sound. Not just because it was a delicious blend of dark and intoxicating but because she was fairly certain he didn't do it in front of most people. She'd somehow breached his outer wall. It was a singular thrill.

He handed her the glass, and their fingers briefly touched. Their eyes connected, but that was also far too brief. He went back to the bookshelf. "To answer your question, I came to get a book."

She sipped from the glass and stifled a sputter as the fiery liquid burned over her tongue and awakened her senses. "You don't have books?"

He turned to look at her. "Of course I do. I've simply read them all."

"All of them?"

He gestured toward the bookshelf. "And unfortunately nearly all of these."

"What of your library at Lakemoor? Have you read all of those too?"

"Not quite. It's rather extensive. You should see it sometime."

How she'd love that, and it had nothing to do with her passion for books. She wanted to see his home. "I would like that. Perhaps I will find a reason to come."

"I just gave you one."

Her lips curved up as she stared at him in bemusement. "You seem to think people can do whatever they want, whenever they want. Life is, unfortunately, not that simple or straightforward for most people."

His eyes narrowed briefly. "No, I suppose it is not. My apologies. You are welcome to visit at any time." He turned back to the bookshelf and set his glass on the edge in front of a particularly thick tome.

She hadn't meant to upset him. "I should like that—doing anything I choose. I could almost do that in St. Ives. No one much cared what I did, and that was rather liberating."

He kept his back to her. "I would

imagine so after being in London. Young women such as yourself are scrutinized in a horrid fashion."

She joined him at the bookshelf. "So are forbidden dukes. It makes one conclude that London, or rather Society, is the problem."

He glanced down at her. "Just so. You would enjoy independence? But of course you would. What fool wouldn't?"

It was her turn to laugh. "I actually think several of the women I met in my earlier Seasons would not. I'm not sure they would know what to do with themselves."

Now he pivoted. He leaned his shoulder against the bookshelf. His gaze caressed her, and she had to fight the urge to sway toward him. "But *you* would. Tell me."

Nora took another sip of whisky. Happily, this swallow went down much more smoothly. "If I could do anything I chose?" At his nod, she continued. "I'd live in the country. I do enjoy some of London's attractions—the museum, for one—but I shouldn't like to be here all of the time. A village would be nice. I adore market days."

"Would you live alone?" He seemed to be genuinely interested.

"I'm not above wanting at least one retainer. Perhaps a married couple—a woman to help with the house and kitchen, and her husband to help with the land and maintenance."

"You've thought this through," he said.

She smiled, enjoying this conversation. Enjoying him. "Just now, actually."

"Besides your retainers, would there be anyone else? A husband, perhaps? I thought that was what you wanted."

She'd thought so too, but now that it seemed within her grasp, she wasn't sure. She kept thinking of her sister. "My sister married the local vicar. She's happy enough, but I don't think she's content." Nora shook her head. "I daresay that makes no sense."

"On the contrary, I understand you perfectly. You don't want to follow in her footsteps. If you're going to marry, you'd like more."

He *did* understand. "I think I might be too old for this endeavor after all. I feel like a bit of an ingrate. Lady Satterfield has been so kind and generous."

The space between them grew smaller. She realized he'd inched forward.

"You mustn't think of it like that. My stepmother will not want you to do anything you don't wish. If you've changed your mind about taking a husband, you must tell her."

Nora was having a hard time focusing on their conversation. His proximity was playing merry hell with her ability to concentrate. "I haven't changed my mind exactly. I just think that I'd rather remain unwed than marry the wrong person."

"You are a wise woman, Nora." He closed his eyes briefly and when they reopened, the green was so sharp and brilliant that Nora nearly blinked. "My apologies, Miss Lockhart. I didn't mean to overstep."

She nearly invited him to do just that, but caught herself before the words tumbled out. She was a bit surprised by her success, since she felt as though she'd fallen into a trance. One she didn't particularly want to emerge from.

"You promised to tell me how you ignore everyone," she said. "Will you tell me now?"

He arched a brow. "It's a well-guarded secret—the very core of my reputation as the Forbidden Duke." He rolled his eyes, shocking her with his behavior. He seemed so...accessible. Not forbidden at all. "It's a nonsensical name."

"But somehow dashing just the same. We want what we can't have, do we not? Calling you forbidden makes you desperately appealing."

He leaned even closer. "Does it?"

Nora's breath was trapped in her chest. Her skin felt aflame. Desire and need pooled in her belly. She managed to keep herself very still despite the riot going on inside of her. "Yes."

"Then for you, I shall be forbidden."

Any prayer she had for keeping her inappropriate thoughts to herself completely fled. "That's a shame, for I was hoping you might kiss me again."

"I was hoping you would ask." He didn't hesitate before his mouth claimed hers. Where he'd gone slowly before, this was much different. His lips were insistent, his tongue seeking immediate entrance. She opened for him and went to clasp his shoulders, but realized she still held her whisky glass.

He seemed to read her mind as his fingers wrapped around hers for a brief moment. He took the glass from her, and she heard a soft clack as he set it on the bookshelf.

His arms came around her waist, and he pulled her flush against his body. Her night rail and night robe were scant protection against the heat and weight of his frame. But she didn't want protection. On the contrary, she wanted to feel him naked against her. She touched his chest and ran her hands up his coat until she found his bare flesh above the collar of his shirt. She curled her fingers around his nape, threading through the silky ends of his hair.

His tongue licked deep into her mouth. Sensation careened through her, sending heat to that space between her legs. No man had ever been closer to her, but it wasn't close enough. She tugged at his hair and pushed into him.

He squeezed her waist, kissing her almost savagely. But oh, it was so wonderful. She'd never imagined such a rush of pleasure, such a bone-deep need.

Suddenly he was gone, stepping back from her. "Nora, this is not a good idea." He stared at her, his lips parted, his breathing ragged.

It was a terrible idea, of course. There were so many reasons she should run upstairs, not the least of which was the fact that he was her benefactress's son or that history could very well repeat itself. Except, this felt different. Haywood had misled her, *deceived* her. With Titus, this felt...right even though Society would damn her for being wrong. "You are, unfortunately, correct. It doesn't matter that I want you—and I do, quite fervently."

She felt no shame, even though Society said she ought. She did, however, feel the pressure of propriety, and that was why she should go. Regardless, her feet were lead, and her mind was tethered to this moment.

His eyes were dark with what she was certain was lust, but also wary. "You are tempting me beyond a man's rational thought."

"I fear my logic fled right around the time you said that you would be forbidden for me. I want what I can't have, Titus. Yes, I'm going to call you Titus if you are to call me Nora."

"It doesn't look or sound as if either one of us is leaving."

Their gazes locked, holding them in place as if they still embraced. Nora couldn't bring herself to compare this to her foolishness nine years ago. Then, she hadn't fully considered the consequences, nor had she experienced this depth of desire or emotion. "I can't seem to drag myself away."

She wanted to be like him, not to care what anyone thought. But could she really throw her future away to spend this night with this man? The words fell out of her mouth as soon as they rushed into her head: "No one will know."

He blinked at her. "What's that?"

"I said, no one will know. What we choose to do here... No one will know.

The entire staff is upstairs asleep, save the footman, who is probably asleep at his post after letting you in." She wouldn't be ruined. Her future could be secure—after everything he'd done for her, she trusted him to ensure that. She repeated herself, but this time with the edge of a query. "No one will know."

He shook his head, and his eyes burned with intense promise. "*Never.*"

"Except us," she said softly, a warm anticipation spreading over her as she made her decision. "I should like for you to stay. Here. With me. And…continue. I am no longer the green girl I was, and I'm aware of the risk I am taking. I don't know what my future holds. I *want* this night. I want *you.*" She trembled with excitement and apprehension. Would he think ill of her? Worse, would he deny her?

"Nora, are you certain? There are things—"

She moved swiftly to the door and turned the lock, thankful that it even had one. Then she stepped toward him and put her finger on his lips. "Shh. I don't wish to speak of them now. I have no expectations of you beyond this night. I'll understand if your honor demands you take your leave, but I would much rather you stay."

He wrapped his hand around hers,

drawing her fingertip from his mouth. "What is honor when compared with this gift? You can have me. But it's your choice. I want you to wield that power."

Oh God, she did.

He unbuttoned his coat with slow, meticulous flicks of his thumb and fingers. He peeled the garment from his shoulders and tossed it to the chair. Then he repeated the act with his waistcoat. When his fingers tugged at his cravat, his gaze turned even darker, and the pupils grew larger. Watching him pull the neck cloth away, exposing the flesh of his throat, she felt like the most powerful woman in the world. This man was hers for the taking.

She'd claim this scrap of independence, of supremacy, and wield it. For the past nine years. For the future and whatever it would bring.

For herself.

She untied the sash at her waist and shrugged the night robe to the floor. Taking a deep breath, she pulled the night rail over her head in a single, rapid movement lest she lose her courage. "Show me what to do." She looked him in the eye, and for a moment, desire stretched between them, became a palpable thing. She held her breath.

"You are beautiful." He took a step

toward her, his gaze moving over her with predatory intent.

She moved her hand to cover herself, but he reached out and stopped her. "Please. Don't. I just want to look. Can I?" He raised his eyes to hers, and she saw stark need, but also courtesy. If she said no, he'd let her go. Of that, she had no doubt.

She let her hand fall to her side and forced herself to relax. There would never be another night like this. She wanted to immerse herself in the experience. In him.

He moved closer, pausing in front of her as his gaze dropped to her chest. Her breasts tingled beneath his stare. She wouldn't think she could feel so sensitive without him touching her. He stepped around to her side—slowly, his gaze probing her in ways she wasn't sure his hands could.

She felt vulnerable, standing naked before him. She'd never been more keenly aroused, had never imagined such a sensation existed.

He moved behind her. She felt his breath against her neck. He was close. But not so close that he touched her. A thrill tickled her spine. Her breasts pulled. She glanced down and saw her nipples had grown hard.

He came around her other side, entering her line of sight once more. His dark head was bent. She caught his sandalwood scent. It only heightened her arousal.

She wanted to look at him the same way he was surveying her. "You're wearing far too many clothes." It was all she could manage. Her voice was made of small, hard pebbles.

"I am." He sat on the edge of the chair and pulled off his boots. His stockings followed as he peeled them off in quick succession.

He stood and pulled the tail of his shirt from his breeches. She went to him and covered his hands with hers. "May I?"

He looked at her, his eyes gleaming like emeralds. "Yes." His hands stilled, then fell to his sides. She drew the shirt up, exposing his flesh. He was unimaginably muscular, the planes of his abdomen sculpted like a statue.

He raised his arms as she pulled the garment over his head. She dropped the linen to the floor, heedless of where it landed. Thoughts fled her brain like bees in a downpour. She was absolutely speechless at his beauty.

Unlike him, however, she couldn't keep herself from touching him. She reached out and caressed her fingertips against the space between his belly and his chest. He was warm and smooth and hard.

He flinched and sharply inhaled.

She snatched her hand away and looked back up at his face.

He found her hand and put it back on his chest, higher this time, where it wasn't smooth, but dusted with dark hair. "Don't stop. Unless you want to."

She didn't want to. She flattened her palm against him, reveling in the feel of his hair and the plane of his flesh beneath.

"Nora," he rasped. "I'd like to touch you too. May I?"

She realized she hadn't asked for permission, but he didn't seem to mind. She was flattered that he'd thought to do that. "Yes. Please."

She tensed, eager but also afraid.

He gently skimmed his fingertips along her shoulder, moving inward to her collarbone then drifting downward between her breasts. She tensed, but his touch was light, deft. He drew his hand through the soft valley then beneath her right breast. His knuckles brushed the underside, and it was her turn to gasp.

His hand curved and came up, cupping her. He was still incredibly gentle, going as slowly as she could ever want.

"Is this difficult for you?" she asked.

"In what way?" He cradled her, his thumb brushing over her breast in ever increasing swaths, bringing him closer and closer to her nipple.

She found herself straining, wanting that touch. Needing that connection. "You're so…controlled. I can barely keep a thought in my head."

"You seem to think I have many, when in fact I have just one—pleasuring you."

Oh God. Her knees quivered, her thighs, all of her took on the properties of a jelly.

He wrapped his arm around her waist and held her. Finally, *finally*, his thumb brushed over her nipple and then the unthinkable happened. He bent and took her into his mouth, his lips closing over her flesh.

She'd kept her hand on him throughout his exploration, but she wanted more. She moved her hand to his head and curled her fingers into his hair. His grip on her waist tightened as he tongued her. The strokes were light at first, teasing, but grew with intensity until he was nearly devouring her with his mouth. Or at least that was how she would describe it. And she could think of no finer characterization, because it made her feel distinctly hungry. For what, she wasn't yet certain, but she knew he would satisfy her. He'd said his only thought was to pleasure her.

She closed her eyes as he feasted, moving

to her other breast. She let her head fall back as she held on to him—one hand twisted into his hair and the other clasping his shoulder. Heat and desire flowed through her until a wild craving built between her thighs. She knew what would happen next, what *could* happen, if she allowed it.

She shouldn't, but why not? This night was for her. He wanted her to have the power of choice, and she chose this.

His mouth left her breast just before his hand cradled her neck. She opened her eyes to see he'd straightened and was looking at her. She thought he might say something, but he didn't. His mouth descended on hers, and his lips and tongue consumed her. This was like no kiss she'd ever imagined. She realized everything about this was beyond her comprehension, and she felt a moment's sadness that she'd existed for twenty-seven years without experiencing this. Another reason to embrace it—him— while she could. She closed her eyes again and let herself dissolve into this moment.

He held her head captive while he pillaged her mouth, his tongue licking, his lips suckling. She tried to mimic what he did, using her tongue, clasping at his flesh, but feared she was a hopeless amateur.

With the hand around her waist, he

pulled her against him. Their chests met, and she moaned into his mouth. Her breasts, already enflamed from his kisses, grew even more sensitive. The sensations in her nipples pulsed through her and settled between her legs, driving her hips forward.

Though he still wore clothing over his lower half, she felt the length of his arousal against her lower belly. Need exploded there, but it wasn't quite right. She stood on her toes, seeking to position him in the right spot. Then he grazed it, and light flickered behind her eyelids.

He broke the kiss and in a fluid movement, picked her up and delivered her to the settee. He laid her gently on the cushions and stared down at her. His jaw was clenched, and she had the sense that he was just barely composed. She wondered if he ever let himself go completely. She wanted to see that.

"Nora, shall I stop?"

"Now? It's just becoming interesting." That flash of pleasure she'd felt hinted at far more to come. There was no way she would allow him to stop. "Show me what to do."

"You are incomparable." A faint smile lifted his lips. He knelt on the cushion near her feet. He clasped the ankle next to the back of the settee and pushed her leg up.

Then he wrapped his hand around the other ankle, his thumb massaging her flesh. "Trust me to give you pleasure. Can you do that?"

She nodded, her body screaming for release. His hand glided up her calf, stroking her softly as he ascended her leg. Her breath came more quickly, and her pulse pounded in her ears. He flattened his palm against her inner thigh and pushed, exposing her most sensitive flesh.

Instinctively she tried to close her legs, but he held her firmly. "Trust me, Nora."

He gripped her leg thus while his right hand moved between her thighs. His fingertips skimmed along her flesh. She bucked her hips, shocked at the intimate contact.

He held her fast and stroked her, eliciting the same sensation she'd felt when she'd pushed against him. But it was over and over again, building. His touch became firmer, his thumb finding a particularly sensitive spot that made her cry out. He leaned over and kissed her again, his mouth open and wet and so wonderful.

She kissed him back, desperate for something to keep her from exploding. His finger slipped inside of her then, and once more, her hips came up off the settee.

He ripped his mouth from hers, and their

ragged breathing filled the room. His hand continued its delicious assault, provoking her into a mindless frenzy. Without intent, her hips rotated into his touch, seeking more.

His breath rushed against her ear. "I want to put my mouth on you. Will you let me?"

She tried to understand his words, but it was nearly impossible for now he was also kissing her neck, ravishing her flesh. She tipped her head back against the cushion and moaned.

"Nora, please."

She clutched at his back, her fingers digging into his flesh and strove to answer. "Your mouth…where?"

His finger plunged into her, and light flashed again behind her eyes. "*Here.*"

Yes, God, yes, whatever he wanted.

She must've spoken out loud because he moved down her body, his mouth leaving a trail of wicked kisses in its wake. When his tongue licked her *there*, she made a ghastly sound. A sound she didn't think a woman could make.

He didn't take his time, nor was he gentle. As with her breasts, he devoured her, his lips and tongue coaxing her into an increasingly fervent state. She thrust up into him, seeking that sweet release she knew must be coming.

He suckled that sensitive spot as his finger stroked into her, and everything inside of her pulled taut. Time seemed to freeze as her body convulsed. Then the world simply exploded.

Chapter Eleven
※·3·※

TITUS FELT HER orgasm wash through her. Her muscles clenched, and moisture flooded his tongue. Her release, the totality of her abandon, was the sweetest thing he'd ever tasted.

His cock throbbed in his breeches. Menswear was simply not meant for lovemaking. He leaned back and watched her as he stroked her through the aftermath. She was, by far, the loveliest woman he'd ever beheld. And it wasn't to do with the pale perfection of her breasts, or the gentle slope of her hip, or the rose hue of her lush lips. It was about her trust in him and her boldness in taking what she wanted.

He'd wanted to give her pleasure, and she'd taken it. Indeed, she'd grabbed it with both hands and met it in the most primal fashion. He was, in a word, enraptured.

But he would stop if she asked him to. He'd done what he'd intended. Far more, actually. He'd come here just to be in the same house as this woman who'd thoroughly enchanted him. He'd never imagined they would come together—and certainly not like this. Which wasn't to say he hadn't fantasized about it. He'd pictured her thus—naked and sprawled before him, her flesh pink from pleasure—far too many times to count.

She opened her eyes and gazed at him in wonder.

He forced himself to speak. "Nora, if you want me to stop, it must be now."

She glanced down at the bulge in his breeches. "What about you?"

"This was never about me. It was about you."

"Then I'm not finished." She sat up and reached for the buttons of his fall. "*We're* not finished."

He clasped her hands, effectively stilling them. "Nora, if we continue, you will no longer be as you are. Do you understand?"

"I am already no longer as I was. And thank *God* for that. Thank God for you." Her brow arched. "If you think I'm letting you leave now, you haven't been paying attention."

He enjoyed the slight narrowing of her eyes, the dark intent in her gaze. "You're rather despotic, aren't you?"

"Yes, if I must be. Titus…"

He watched her search for the words to

say what she wanted and decided to rescue her. "If you insist."

"I do." She pushed his hand away and continued with his buttons until his breeches gapped open. Then she tugged at the garment. "Off."

He stood and stripped his clothing away until he stood nude before her. He expected her gaze to affix on his hardened cock and wasn't disappointed. He was surprised however, and perhaps shouldn't have been, when she reached out and ran her fingertips along his length.

She sucked in a breath and continued to stare at him as a bead of moisture formed at the tip. She stroked him again and tentatively touched the drop. She glanced up at him. "What does it taste like?"

He tried not to laugh and failed. "I'm sure I don't know."

She nodded slowly as her gaze dropped once more. "Your flesh is much softer than I imagined." She curled her fingers around him, instinctively knowing what to do to please him. At least, he assumed it was instinct.

"Nora, you are inexplicably expert at this."

"Am I?" She continued caressing his shaft, and he couldn't stop his hips from snapping forward. He'd been on the verge of orgasm when he'd pushed her over the edge, but had managed to keep a handle on himself. "There it is again," she murmured. Then her head tipped forward, and her tongue darted out to catch the next drop that had beaded on the head.

"Good God, Nora, you are going to kill me."

"Hmmm, salty. More of…that comes out…later?"

"When I have an orgasm, yes. Like you did."

"But this could make me with child." She frowned. Her hand continued its slow but wondrous torture. "That would be a problem."

Hell yes, it would. "There are precautions," he said tightly. "Not infallible, but nothing is."

"Then you shall employ them." She tightened her grip, unwittingly sending him even closer to the edge. "Let us continue."

"We have been this entire time. Have you no inkling what you've been doing to me?"

She arched that damned brow again. "I'm not a simpleton."

"No, by God, you are not."

He pushed her back on the settee and settled himself between her legs. "Please forgive me my gracelessness. I have absolutely no experience with virgins."

"I think you have an inaccurate perspective as to how this encounter has progressed. If you haven't noticed, I'm enjoying myself immensely. And I don't expect that to change. You are far too considerate." She pulled at his hips. "Please, Titus. Just do remember to take whatever precautions are necessary."

Yes, he would need to keep his wits about him. The second his cock touched her, he feared he was lost. He guided himself inside her, unsure of what to expect. She was unfathomably tight. Her muscles gripped his shaft as he slid slowly into her slick passage.

He teased her clitoris, sensing her tense the farther he intruded. He coaxed her flesh, stirring her until he felt her relax. Then he pushed himself to the hilt.

He leaned forward and brushed his lips against her temple. "Are you uncomfortable?"

"No. This is…pleasant, actually. That feeling I had before, the sensation that I might rip in two… I fear it might be returning."

Fear? "You didn't like it?"

"Oh no, I *adored* it."

Incomparable indeed.

He began to move, slowly at first. He didn't want to hurt her. Soon, she was moving with him, her hips arcing up. The friction was beyond spectacular. He wasn't going to last long but suspected that was for the best. If he could just bring her with him…

He found her clitoris again and worked her flesh until her movements became more emphatic. She thrust with him, the room filling with the sounds of their bodies coming together.

He drove faster, and his orgasm sped to its conclusion. "Come with me, Nora." He vaguely realized she had no idea what he meant, but then it happened. She cried out, and her muscles constricted around him. His balls tightened, and he just barely managed to pull out before he spilled inside of her. Instead, he came on her belly, which was, as he'd feared, rather graceless.

Powerless to do anything but empty his seed, he stroked his shaft until he was complete. Satisfaction—bone-deep and toe-curling—pitched through him. But what a mess.

"See, I said you would need to forgive me." He moved away from her and found his discarded cravat. Then he returned and wiped her flesh clean.

"Better there than in the other…place," she said, showing a sense he found devastatingly attractive. Along with everything else about her.

He helped her sit up, then presented her with her night clothes. While she covered herself, he set about conducting his own toilet. His valet would cringe at the state of his clothing, but Titus didn't care. This had been the best night he could recall in a ridiculously long time. Maybe in the entirety of his life.

"That   was…astonishing."   Her declaration seemed to mirror his thoughts, sending a jolt of pleasure through him.

"Indeed."

She stood from the settee and tied the sash around her night robe. "You are still a man of few words."

He sat on the chair to pull on his stockings and boots. "I thought I spoke plenty."

Her answering smile was devilish, and he knew in that moment that he'd never be able to look at her again without thinking of this encounter, of what they'd shared. No matter what happened, they were connected on a level he'd never experienced.

"You did, actually," she said. "Quite shockingly. I do thank you for taking those…precautions. But mostly, I must thank you for allowing me to satisfy my curiosity."

Hopefully it meant more to her than that. It had to him. "Is that what this was, an experiment?"

She lifted a shoulder. "Not that, but maybe a question for which I had no answer until now."

He loved how her mind worked. "And what is the answer?"

"That I can trust myself to choose what I want. That maybe what I thought I wanted isn't. You've given me much to think about. I guess I maybe don't have the actual answer yet. Perhaps this is a conversation we can have another time." She yawned, which seemed to punctuate her statement.

She leaned forward and kissed his cheek, surprising him. It was a sweet gesture. No one had done that except his stepmother. It made him feel…safe.

"Good night, Titus. Sleep well." She went to the door and opened it, looking over her shoulder before she left. "I know I shall."

He watched her go and fetched the whisky glasses from the shelf. He frowned and wondered if anyone would make note of the fact that there were two of them and try to puzzle who'd they'd belonged to. No one knew he was here, save the night footman who'd been dozing under the stairs when he'd arrived.

He tossed back the contents of both glasses and deposited them on the sideboard, then made his way from the house.

Outside, the predawn was dark, the city as quiet as it could ever be. He roused his coachman and directed him to drive home.

As he reclined in the interior, casting his head back against the squab, he marveled at how blissfully sated he felt. At the same time, a splinter of discomfort wedged into his brain. He hadn't taken advantage of her, and yet he'd ruined her just the same. She could still marry, and probably would, but he'd taken that which she should've given to her husband.

A tiny voice in his head asked why that couldn't be him.

Marry her. Make her his duchess. His *forbidden* duchess. He smiled at that thought.

His smile faded. Would she want that? Tonight's events had affected her greatly. Even before they'd made love, she'd talked about an independent life with the fervor of one who desperately wanted something they didn't think they could have.

He'd heard enough about her background from his stepmother to know that she was financially destitute and basically homeless. Her father seemed a feckless sort, and Titus wanted to know why he hadn't planned better for his daughter.

As the coach neared his town house, he was no closer to determining what he should do next. Maybe because the next move was hers. He'd wanted to give her power tonight—choice—and he didn't want to take it from her.

Marry her, his mind said.

Perhaps he could offer her another one.

NORA WAS THRILLED to have a day of respite. She was exhausted. Though she'd felt tired after her encounter with Titus, she hadn't been able to sleep. Her mind and body had been too overcome with thought and sensation. She wished they could have lain together in bed, side by side, and talked until the dawn.

In the afternoon, she and Lady Satterfield sat together in the upstairs sitting room enjoying tea. Lady Satterfield was reading, and Nora was writing a letter to her sister. She couldn't quite find the words to tell Jo what had happened with Titus and longed to see her in person.

Harley entered the sitting room. "Lord Markham is here to call on Miss Lockhart."

Lady Satterfield set her book down. "Indeed?" She glanced excitedly at Nora before looking back to Harley. "Do show him into the drawing room. We'll be there in a moment."

Nora set down her pen and checked her hands for ink stains. She looked down at her day dress. It was appropriate for callers, but she hadn't really prepared herself for visitors since this had been a planned day of rest.

Lady Satterfield seemed to read Nora's thoughts. "You look splendid, dear."

Nora considered asking the countess to tell Lord Markham that they weren't receiving callers today, but it was too late for that. Besides, Nora loved seeing Lady Satterfield's excitement.

Nora patted the back of her hair, which was swept up into a simple chignon. "Is my hair all right?"

"As I said, you look splendid. Come, let's not keep the earl waiting." Lady Satterfield stood and went to the door, which Harley had left ajar.

Nora followed her into the drawing room.

Lord Markham was dressed in riding clothes, his buff breeches hugging him with a perfect fit. Nora couldn't help but notice he didn't fill out his costume quite as well as Titus, but then she doubted anyone could. And now that she'd seen and felt Titus without any adornment, she felt thoroughly qualified to make such judgments. Even if they were scandalously inappropriate.

Markham offered a smart bow to both Nora and the countess. He rose with a smile. "Good afternoon, Lady Satterfield, Miss Lockhart. It's lovely to see you today." Though the comment was likely for both of them, his intent stare made it seem as if he were speaking only to Nora.

She responded with a curtsey. "And you, Your Grace. I am delighted that you've come." She wished she could feel even the slightest thrill at his obvious interest in her. Oh, it was flattering and charming, but it didn't ignite her soul the way one look from Titus could do.

"I wanted to thank you for the dance last night," he said.

Had that just been last night? Because of what had happened after, Nora was positive it had to be the more distant past. But of course it wasn't.

"Will you be in the park later? Perhaps we can promenade." He looked quite hopeful, and for a fleeting moment, Nora considered changing her mind about staying home the rest of the day.

She offered a warm smile. "Actually, we're going to have a quiet afternoon and evening, but I do thank you for the invitation. Another day?"

He nodded. "Indeed. I do hope you'll attend Lady Burney's soiree night after next. Lady Burney is my sister."

Nora flicked a glance at Lady Satterfield. She couldn't recall what their calendar held for the remainder of the week. It seemed last night's events had turned her into a featherwit.

Lady Satterfield returned a subtle nod, causing Nora to answer, "Yes. We're looking forward to it."

He smiled brightly. "Excellent. I shall hope for the first dance. I shall take my leave. I wish you a restorative day, Miss Lockhart." He offered another bow and again when he rose, his eyes seemed to bore into hers.

As he bowed to Lady Satterfield next, Harley entered. The butler looked to the countess and said, "Mr. Dawson is here, my lady."

Lord Markham straightened, and a flicker of some emotion—a shadow of disappointment perhaps—passed over his expression. He quickly covered the momentary lapse before offering them both a final smile and departing the room.

"Show him in, Harley." Lady Satterfield turned to Nora. "My goodness. Two suitors in one day. And they'll see each other in passing." Her eyes twinkled with glee. "Oh, this could become quite fun!"

A decade ago, maybe even five years ago, Nora would have agreed. Now, however, the notion made her feel slightly queasy. She liked Markham and Dawson, but when she compared them to Titus... She had to stop doing that!

Except she couldn't. What had been a fantasy—an infatuation—in her mind, had become reality last night, if only for a short time. She'd caught a glimpse of what it was like to be held in Titus's arms, and she feared anyone else would fall far too short.

Mr. Dawson stalked forward, his smile broad and engaging. He bowed first to Lady Satterfield. "Good afternoon, my lady, thank you for your kind hospitality."

"Good afternoon, Mr. Dawson, the pleasure is ours." She inclined her head and angled her body toward Nora.

Dawson moved to Nora and bowed a trifle more elegantly. When he straightened, his gaze was captivatingly straightforward. Nora liked this man's simplicity and artlessness.

"Good afternoon, Miss Lockhart." His tone carried a softer edge than when he'd spoken to Lady Satterfield. "I am so pleased to find you at home. I wonder if we might take a stroll around the garden?" He looked toward the countess. "If Lady Satterfield permits."

"Of course." She nodded. "Just go through there and take the stairs down from the terrace. I'll follow you and sit in the library where I can see you."

So Nora was allowed to take an unchaperoned walk with Titus, but not with Mr. Dawson? Perhaps that was because Lady Satterfield had no reason to believe that Titus was interested in Nora in any other capacity beyond helping her successfully navigate the Season.

Mr. Dawson offered his arm. "Shall we?"

Nora placed her hand on his sleeve, and they walked through the rear sitting room onto the terrace. She instantly noted that Dawson's arm lacked the strength and substance of Titus's. He also lacked Titus's ruggedly masculine scent and the simple aura of potent virility that seemed to follow Titus. Oh, heavens, she was a ninny! She sounded like a lovestruck girl.

She nearly tripped on the stairs as they descended to the garden.

That's because she *was* a lovestruck girl.

She was in love with Titus. What has started as an impossible fancy, an unattainable dream had become her most fervent desire. He made her feel comfortable, strong, and special. She'd never felt those things before.

"It's a particularly fine day, though I do worry about the clouds I saw on the horizon. It may not be quite so pleasant by five o'clock."

Nora forced herself to pay attention to what Dawson was saying. "Yes," was all she could manage for an answer while her mind—and heart—struggled to make sense of what she'd just realized.

"I do miss the country," he said. "As do you."

They'd discussed that very topic last night during their dance. He had a modest house in Sussex where he enjoyed fishing and walking with his two boys, aged five and seven. Nora had warmed to the obvious love he felt for them. She didn't doubt she could be happy there. As happy as she'd been in St. Ives at least and probably more so.

"Yes. I admit this rigorous schedule is a bit overwhelming. In fact, Lady Satterfield and I are enjoying a restful pause today."

He turned his head and looked at her in dismay. "And here I've spoiled it. I should have called another day."

She didn't want him to feel bad. "It's

quite all right."

He continued along the path, which circuited the small garden. "I suppose so, since you also accepted Markham's call."

Was there a note of annoyance or perhaps jealousy in his voice? She decided to ignore it if there was.

He cleared his throat. "Might I ask… That is… Do I need to worry about my competition?"

Well, that was about as declarative as he'd been regarding his intentions. "There's no competition, Mr. Dawson."

"You undervalue yourself, Miss Lockhart. You've become quite popular. I fear my chances for your hand are dwindling." He drew her to a halt behind a shrubbery so that they were partially obscured from Lady Satterfield's view from the library window. He turned and looked at her earnestly. "Let me be clear that I am in pursuit of your hand."

Nora winced inwardly. He was so kind, so dear. Yet, she couldn't stop herself from longing for a different man, one who was not interested in marriage. She ought to be clear with Mr. Dawson, except he might be her only chance for the future she wanted.

She wasn't certain how to respond. She didn't want to give him false hope, not when her mind was churning. "I am so honored by your attention, Mr. Dawson. Truly. However, I am not yet ready to made a decision about my future."

"I understand. I'm quite patient." He glanced toward the house and when he looked back, the edge of his mouth twisted briefly, as if he were chewing the inside of his lip. Something about his demeanor belied what he'd said about patience.

Nora started walking again, eager to put an end to this interview so that she could be alone with her thoughts. There had never been a better day for her and Lady Satterfield to withdraw. "I appreciate your understanding. You've given me much to ponder."

"I hope you'll agree that we are exceptionally well suited. I shan't find a finer woman to raise my sons."

His words speared sharply into her heart. It wasn't an outright proposal, but she was certain one would be forthcoming. She quickened her pace until they reached the library. Lady Satterfield went to the bookshelf, partially turning her back, presumably giving them a moment of half-privacy before Mr. Dawson took his leave.

He took her hand and pressed a kiss to the back. "I do hope you'll think on what I said. I look forward to seeing you soon." He bowed, then turned to Lady Satterfield.

"Good afternoon, my lady."

"Good afternoon," she murmured. Then he strode from the room.

Lady Satterfield waited until he was gone before going to Nora. Her eyes were bright with anticipation. "What did he say?"

Nora didn't wish to provide all the details. Not right now while her thoughts were a jumble. Dawson would make a good husband. Why couldn't she want him as much as she wanted Titus? "Only that he wishes to call on me again."

"Do you think a proposal is at hand?"

Most certainly, but again, Nora didn't wish to discuss the particulars. Not until she wrapped her mind around falling in love with Titus and accepting that a future with him would never come to pass.

But why not?

Because he hadn't once discussed a future or any intent to marry—either her or anyone else. And even if he had, could she really be his duchess? Over the past several days, she'd come to realize this life wasn't really for her. She preferred the quiet of the country, the independence of living on her own terms, even if it meant she was lonely. But with someone like Dawson, she didn't have to be lonely. No, with someone like Dawson, she could perhaps have everything she desired. Everything except love, or at least passion. And while she might not want to live without that, there were far worse things.

Lady Satterfield clasped her hands together. "Well, there is no denying it now, my dear, you are the toast! With both Markham and Dawson paying calls, I daresay your future is secure."

Nora realized she'd never answered her question, but supposed it didn't matter. Lady Satterfield was pleased and happy for Nora, and that made Nora happy.

Yes, her future was secure. The only question was whether it was the future she truly wanted.

Chapter Twelve

THE FOLLOWING DAY, Titus went to his club for luncheon before the House of Lords session. His stepmother was hosting a tea that afternoon, but he didn't have time to attend. Nora had been at the forefront of his thoughts, and he planned to see her soon. Perhaps he'd stop in tonight after the session finished.

As he walked through the dining room, he saw Mr. Jonathan Gasper, a horse breeder with excellent stock, sitting by himself. Seeing him here, Titus was struck with the rather spontaneous urge to speak with him about a horse for Nora. Before he could make his way to Gasper's table, a footman approached him.

"Your Grace, I'll have your usual luncheon sent up directly."

Titus appreciated the footman's care. "I'm going to speak with someone first. Do wait a bit."

The footman hesitated the briefest moment before saying, "As you say, Your Grace." He began to turn, but Titus stopped him.

"And I think I'd prefer mutton today."

The footman's nostrils flared. It was a slight thing, but Titus caught the reaction. "Indeed, Your Grace."

Titus had known this particular footman for quite a while. He knew Titus's habits and preferences, and Titus had just surprised him. Twice.

Absurdly, Titus was amused. He felt good. Yes, for the first time in a very long time, he felt *good*.

He made his way to Gasper. "Afternoon, Gasper, I wonder if I might have a word."

The gentleman looked up from his soup and blinked. "Kendal. Yes, yes, of course." He gestured for Titus to sit. "Are you having luncheon?"

Why not eat it here instead of his private dining room? "Yes, do you mind if I join you?"

Gasper studied him for a moment. "Not at all." It seemed he might say something more, but he took another spoonful of soup instead.

"I wanted to speak with you about acquiring a new mount—a gentle mare, something appropriate for a novice rider." Titus signaled for the footman to come to the table.

"How may I be of service, Your Grace?"

"I'll take my luncheon here, thank you." He turned back to Gasper, effectively dismissing the footman, but not before registering that he'd surprised the man a third time.

Titus glanced at the footman's departing back before returning his attention to Gasper. "I'm upsetting the order of things today."

Gasper swallowed another spoonful of soup and set his utensil down. "Because you're eating here?"

"It's not expected, is it?"

Gasper blinked. "No."

He seemed as hesitant and cautious as the footman had been. Was Titus so fearsome? No, but he'd created a wall around himself and preferred that no one breach it save his inner circle. Today, however, he felt like lowering that wall. Just a bit.

He turned the conversation back to horses, and after a while, the footman delivered his meal along with Gasper's next course. They enjoyed a pleasant luncheon, and before Titus realized it, he needed to be on his way.

He was about to excuse himself when two gentlemen strolled by. "I can't believe she chose Dawson," one of them said. "My money was on Markham."

The other man shook his head. "Why'd she choose Dawson over an earl? Makes no sense to me, but then women never do."

Titus stood. "What are you discussing?"

The pair stopped in their tracks and slowly turned. They regarded Titus as if he had a second head. The first man swallowed. "Your Grace?"

Titus's gut clenched. "What are you talking about? Who?" He feared he knew the answer and, like these men, he could make absolutely no sense of it.

"A wager was placed last night at White's. About Miss Lockhart—your stepmother's ward, I believe." The man sounded a bit nervous, tentative. "There seems to be a competition for her hand between Lord Markham and Mr. Dawson."

A bloody competition? A wager? The room seemed to darken, and Titus's breath squeezed from his chest. "You said she chose Dawson?"

The two men exchanged puzzled looks. "Evidently," the second one answered. "We just heard it down at Key's Coffee House."

The good mood Titus had just enjoyed, the only contentment he'd found in nine long years, evaporated like smoke.

Without a word, he turned and strode from the club, his feet devouring the ground as he made his way to his coach. He barely spared a glance for the coachman, who held the door for him. "Satterfield House."

Once inside the vehicle, he exhaled his pent-up breath. She'd chosen Dawson? After what had happened between them the other night?

Well, why wouldn't she, you ass? It's not as if you proposed.

And he should have. Not because it was the right and honorable thing to do, which of course it was, and which *of course* she deserved. But because he loved her. He was irrevocably, hopelessly, desperately in love with her.

He had to tell her. Even if nothing came of it, he had to share what was in his heart before it was too late. He'd lost one person in his life—his father—without telling him how much he meant, and he wasn't going to make that same mistake again.

Chapter Thirteen
❦

DESPITE A BLISSFULLY quiet night at home, Nora was no closer to making a decision about her future. The tea was due to start shortly, and presumably both Markham and Dawson would make an appearance. Neither would ask for her hand during such an occasion, but they would likely press their potential courtships.

She told herself that was fine. Better than fine. Either would be an excellent match, and Dawson had certainly laid out his advantages yesterday.

The mystery lay with Titus. Only there really wasn't a mystery at all. They'd enjoyed a spectacular evening together where no promises were exchanged. She ought to continue as if it had never happened.

She practically choked at the thought.

Another option had skipped into her brain last night as she'd tried to fall asleep. What if she didn't marry anyone? What if she worked as a companion as she'd intended and saved her pennies so that she could afford to retire to the country by herself? Granted, it would take years. And years. But what else did she have to do?

However, on her own she couldn't look forward to a repeat of what she'd experienced with Titus. Which led her back to her choices of husband and the conclusion that she didn't trust that any other man could give her what Titus had. It went far beyond the physical sensations he'd aroused. He'd gifted her with a sense of empowerment, something she'd never even conceived of.

She'd lost everything that mattered nine years ago—her reputation, her ability to secure her future, her ability to secure her sister's future. Two nights ago, she'd realized that she'd actually lost far more: her self-respect. Titus had shown her that she'd regained it and so much more.

Nora walked into the drawing room as Lady Satterfield checked over a table laden with delicate cakes and neat sandwiches. She glanced sideways at Nora. "There you are. Just in time." She straightened, inclining her head toward the door. "They are arriving."

Over the next quarter hour, Nora greeted guests, including Lady Dunn, whose company she'd come to enjoy. The older woman was quite pleased to see that Nora was enjoying a surge in popularity. She clearly took a small amount of credit, since she'd championed Nora from the start.

Lady Dunn nodded toward the doorway. "Your Mr. Dawson is here."

Nora bit her tongue before she said he wasn't *her* Mr. Dawson. She turned in her chair and made eye contact. He instantly smiled and cut toward her.

He took her hand and dropped a kiss to the back. "Good afternoon, Miss Lockhart. You are lovelier than the sun."

"Thank you. I'm delighted you could come today."

He looked at her expectantly. "Might I take you for a turn about the room?"

Nora preferred to continue visiting with Lady Dunn but didn't wish to be rude. "Certainly."

At the precise moment Nora turned to thank Lady Dunn for coming, there was a stir. Conversation picked up in both speed and volume about the room. A woman whose name Nora couldn't quite recall came toward her. Her eyes were wide and animated, her lips curved into an expectant smile.

"May I offer my congratulations to you both," she said, beaming at Nora and Dawson.

Nora looked at Mr. Dawson and saw that he was grinning. What did he have to grin about? Something to do with this mysterious congratulations. A knot formed in Nora's chest.

Dawson sidled closer, his smile appearing perhaps a bit forced upon closer inspection. He looked at Nora intently, his gaze piercing as if he were trying to impart some dire piece of information without saying a word. Then he turned his attention to the woman. "Thank you, Lady Faversham."

"Have you set a wedding date?" Lady Faversham asked.

"What's this?" Lady Dunn asked. She looked between Nora and Dawson. "There's to be a wedding?" Her gaze fixed on Nora, and there was a bit of an accusation in its depths. "I didn't realize you were betrothed." She was angry that Nora hadn't told her. But there hadn't been anything to tell.

Nora opened her mouth, but Dawson's elbow grazed her side as he rushed to answer, "Yes, a wedding. Thank you for your felicitations." He tipped his head down to address Lady Dunn. "Yes, we became betrothed yesterday."

They had done no such thing! Did he somehow think an agreement had been reached when they'd walked around the garden? He couldn't have. She'd given him no assurances, let alone an answer to a proposal he hadn't uttered.

She turned her head to glare at him and saw something in his eyes that gave her pause—fear. What was going on here? Why was he doing this?

Dawson took her hand, and she instinctively tried to snatch it away. He squeezed her fingers, tugging until she looked at him. He leaned slightly forward and whispered, "Please just go along with me. I promise it will all turn out right. Trust me."

Trust him? All the power she'd felt last night leached away, leaving her cold and hopeless. People clamored around them, and the chatter in the drawing room had reached a near-deafening crescendo.

And then it quite simply stopped.

Heads swiveled to the doorway. Standing on the threshold, his face as dark as a storm cloud, was Titus.

The knot in Nora's chest loosened upon seeing him, but then promptly tightened again as she registered his anger. He knew about the betrothal. Which wasn't even real.

She stared at him, hoping to do what Dawson had tried—communicate without saying anything. She tried to convey that she wasn't betrothed, that she didn't want Dawson. Yes, she knew in that moment that she wouldn't accept him or Markham or anyone else. Not when she wanted Titus. She pulled her hand from Dawson's grip and edged away from him.

Titus didn't break eye contact as he strode slowly into the room. People backed away from his path, and still no one spoke. He didn't stop until he was about three feet in front of Nora.

Dawson tried to take her hand again and whispered, "Let's take a walk."

She kept her gaze locked with Titus, urging him to do something. Say *something*.

Titus held his arm out. "Walk with me."

She put her hand on his sleeve, and they walked straight back through the sitting room toward the terrace. Once outside, he closed the door behind them. This might cause a scandal, but then this entire event seemed destined to ruin her newfound status. She couldn't have cared less.

Titus moved away from her and walked to the edge of the terrace that looked out over the garden below. He turned, his face only slightly less fierce than it had been when he arrived. "Tell me what happened."

"I don't know."

"Are you betrothed to him?" The question was harsh, clipped.

"No."

"Then why does all of London think you are?"

"Because he told them?" She took a deep breath and tried to shake the consternation from her head. "He only just arrived a few minutes ago. Someone else—Lady Faversham—congratulated us on our betrothal. I don't know how she heard about it. I do know that he said to her that we became engaged yesterday. He paid me a call, and we strolled around the garden. He made his intent to court me quite clear, but he didn't ask me to wed him."

Titus leaned back against the rail on the terrace. He massaged the bridge of his nose for a moment, then dropped his hand and fixed her with his emerald gaze. "What do you want?"

Her mind was in total disarray. Everything was happening so fast. "What do you mean?"

"Do you wish to marry Dawson? I thought you might prefer a different life— perhaps even without a husband. I know you value your autonomy."

Nora began to relax. Here was the man who understood her. "No, I don't want to marry him, but he's made an awful mess. If I say we aren't betrothed, I will be the one to suffer."

"You are not going to suffer. I promise you that." The simple clarity in his gaze made her believe his words. If anyone could keep her safe, she knew it was Titus.

She tensed again, but with anticipation instead of anxiety. "How?"

He strode toward her and took her hands in his. "They talk about me, they paint me as something I'm not. I ignore them. I've created a façade to keep them at bay. You can do that too. As my wife. Marry me, Nora, and I will give you whatever you want—even if it isn't me."

Oh, but she wanted him. Desperately. But did he want her, or was he simply being the most gallant man she'd ever met?

The door opened, and Dawson stepped out onto the terrace. He looked between them, his gaze landing on their joined hands. He frowned deeply. "You choose him?"

Nora looked at Titus with love bursting in her heart. "I do."

Dawson's answering laugh was surprisingly cold. "Do you know what you've chosen? I would have given you respectability and comfort, a family and security, but you prefer the man who saw you ruined all those years ago."

Darkness crept into Nora's happiness, dulling the edges. She looked at Titus but asked Dawson, "What are you talking about?"

It was Titus who answered, however. "He's talking about Haywood and how I encouraged him to pursue the foolish girl who thought he would marry her. I told him to take whatever he could get away with, that no one would ever find out."

Suddenly she recalled the Marquess of Ravenglass. He'd been the leader of the group Haywood had run with. He was the quintessential Untouchable whose reputation made him almost unacceptable. *Almost.* But not entirely, because he was, after all, the heir to a dukedom. And everyone knew a future duke could do whatever he pleased, including leading idiot young bucks to do the same.

She knew without a doubt that what Dawson said was true. All she had to do was look at the shadow stealing over Titus's face and the regret creeping into his gaze.

Disappointment swirled through her. "You encouraged Haywood. Did you remember who I was from the start?"

His mouth was tight, unyielding. "I did."

"Is that why you helped me? Is what why Lady Satterfield is sponsoring me?"

"*No.*" His response was immediate and vehement. Emotion stormed into his eyes. "Yes, I felt guilty, but when I learned whom she'd hired as her companion, I welcomed the opportunity to right the wrong I'd done you. Yes, I wanted to help you." His gaze softened. "Only I never imagined you'd be the one to save me."

She'd saved him? She wasn't entirely sure what he meant, but the sentiment was so lovely and so pure, she knew Titus wasn't at all the man he'd been nine years ago. And neither was she the same naïvely innocent girl. Right now, with Titus, she could put the past to rest at last. She could be the woman she longed to be—a woman with a choice.

She looked between the two men. The hope and vulnerability in Titus's eyes, coupled with the power to choose, which he was once again ensuring she possessed, made her decision quite simple.

She turned her head to look at Dawson and said, simply, "Yes, I choose Titus."

◆℮•3•◆

TITUS HAD WATCHED the joy fade from her face after Dawson had spilled the truth. Now he stared at her, uncertain of what he was seeing.

"Titus."

The single word came from the doorway. His stepmother had followed them and had clearly heard everything Dawson had said. The anguish in her tone cut straight to his soul. It was like watching his father lose his faith in Titus all over again.

Dawson scoffed. "Of course you'd choose a duke over me."

Titus's stepmother moved onto the terrace. "She chose the better man, you dolt. You should take the stairs down to the garden and escape that way. If you don't, I fear you'll be eaten alive by everyone in the drawing room. The second they find out that Nora is betrothed to my son, you'll be a laughingstock."

Dawson pursed his lips and gave Nora a final beseeching look. "I didn't want to lose you to Markham." He shot a perturbed glance toward Titus. "I didn't even realize he was in the hunt too." He turned his attention back to Nora. "My apologies. I shall be gracious in defeat. I wish you both well."

Nora smiled at him, which was more than he deserved. "Thank you. I wish you the best as well."

Titus marveled at her poise and her generosity of spirit. If he hadn't already been head over heels in love with her, he would be now.

Dawson turned and left.

The countess cleared her throat. "This is

going to cause quite an uproar. The mess Dawson created was exciting enough, but I fear this may break the entire ton."

Titus looked at Nora. The love he felt for her threatened to surge from his chest like a living, breathing thing. A veritable dragon of emotion, the likes of which he'd never encountered. "I don't care."

"No, I'm sure you don't," his stepmother said. "However, Nora may feel differently."

Nora didn't look away from Titus. She stroked his hands with her thumbs. "Actually, I don't. If I'm to be the Forbidden Duchess, I don't need to care about anything. At least not about anything I don't want to. And I choose not to. Titus, I may never hold a ball. Is that all right with you?"

"It only makes me love you more."

Her mouth curved into a smile that was equal parts joyful and seductive. Titus wanted nothing more than to have her alone.

Nora turned to look at the countess. "Must we go back inside?"

His stepmother shook her head gently, her expression resigned but happy. "No. I'll make your excuses. Titus, I regret to inform you that your notoriety will only soar, not that you'll pay any attention to it."

He pulled Nora closer. "Not a bit." He

bent and inhaled the floral fragrance of her hair before pressing a kiss to her temple.

His stepmother smiled widely. "You've made me very happy. Both of you." She turned and went back into the house, closing the door behind her.

Nora looked up at him. "Did you mean what you said? About loving me?"

"Yes. I'm sorry I didn't tell you sooner. I think I realized it the other night. It just… It took me by surprise. I'm not good at this sort of thing." Loving people. Letting them get close.

"I know. You hold yourself so apart from everyone. Is it because of what happened with Haywood?"

He could scarcely understand her compassion. "I wanted to tell you. I just didn't know how. You should be furious with me. I had a hand in ruining you."

"You were young and foolish—like me. What did you mean when you said I'd saved you?"

"I hated myself after what happened to you. Not just because of how it affected you, but because of the disappointment I caused my father. He died shortly after that, and I was, quite simply, wrecked. I've been doing penance all these years. Helping you, loving you has set me free."

Tears glistened in her eyes. "Oh Titus, I

feel precisely the same."

He brushed a fingertip along her cheek. "I wish my father had known you. He would've liked you immensely."

She grinned. "I'm sure the sentiment would've been quite mutual."

"Are you certain you won't mind being the Forbidden Duchess? You were the most celebrated woman in town for a moment."

She laughed. "Yes, my brief time in the sun. Only, I don't need the sun when I have you. You're all I want, Titus. All I need. I love you."

He pulled her into his arms and kissed her full on the mouth. She kissed him back, igniting his desire. He decided right then that a special license would definitely be in order.

After a long moment, he lifted his lips from hers and looked into her eyes. "I've waited my entire life for you, and I'd wait a thousand more. You've made me the happiest man alive. Do you think they'll start calling me the Smitten Duke?"

She giggled. "I don't care what they call you, so long as everyone understands you're *my* duke."

He bent his head to kiss her again. "For eternity."

Epilogue
❧❦❧

London, 1816

WHILE SOME THINGS had changed over the past five years—the most important being the addition of Nora and Titus's two children—many things had not. Lady Satterfield still hosted the first major event of the Season, and Titus still only danced the first dance, though only with Nora. And Nora went to the ball early to help her mother-in-law prepare.

As she entered the ballroom, Nora was struck with a familiar sense of nostalgia. Every year she recalled the night that had changed her life. The night she'd started falling hopelessly in love with her husband.

She smiled as she thought of him at home reading to their children. He'd come to the ball in a little while, in plenty of time for their dance.

Lady Satterfield strode into the drawing room, which had once again been transformed to a glittering ballroom and would soon be filled with Society's finest. Titus and Nora kept to themselves for the most part, but they weren't hermits. Nora attended many events with Lady Satterfield during the Season, but her primary focus was always her family. She paid little attention to the ton, and supposed that in the process, she'd become what she once mocked—an Untouchable. However, not in the sense one might think. She was untouchable because she'd learned not to care what people said or thought. And it was a blissfully freeing state of mind.

"Nora, you look lovely as always," Lady Satterfield said before giving her a quick hug. They exchanged kisses on the cheek, and Nora returned the compliment. "How are my grandchildren?" the countess asked eagerly. She saw them several times a week.

"Very well. They are enjoying the solitary attentions of their father at present."

Lady Satterfield smiled warmly. "He just dotes on them. His father would be so proud."

Though Nora had never known him, she agreed wholeheartedly. Titus had spent far too long bearing the guilt of not living up to his father's expectations, and of not telling him how much he'd loved him. He'd finally found a way to forgive himself, and he credited Nora. However, she believed that they'd conquered those old demons together.

The first guest arrived just then—Lady Dunn with her new companion. The elderly viscountess now walked with a cane, but she was as alert and sharp as always. Nora greeted her along with Lady Satterfield.

"It's always a delight to see you, Your Grace," Lady Dunn said. She seemed to take special pleasure in addressing Nora since she'd become a duchess.

Nora bussed the woman's soft cheek. "You look especially lively this evening."

"You may credit my new companion." Lady Dunn inclined her head to the tall young woman standing just behind her. "This is Miss Ivy Breckenridge. She suggested this concoction in my hair."

The "concoction" consisted of a feather and some flowers. It gave her the height she always sought—Lady Dunn was rather petite and often employed a feather to make her appear taller—as well as a splash of youthful charm due to the posies.

"It's lovely," Nora said. She looked at Miss Breckenridge, whose expression was impassive. "Well done."

The companion nodded slightly. "Thank you. Come, Lady Dunn, we must get you settled."

"Yes, yes, a chair would not come amiss."

"We've just the spot for you in the sitting room, with a perfect view of the dancing through the open doorway," Nora said, leading them from the ballroom and leaving Lady Satterfield to join her husband in order to greet their guests.

Within the next half hour, the rooms were nearly full with the usual crush. The dancing would soon begin, which meant that Titus would sneak in the back just in time to dance with her. Nora smiled to herself in anticipation as her feet carried her toward the open terrace doors.

She caught sight of three young women standing in the corner, one of whom was the enigmatic Miss Breckenridge, whom she'd met earlier. The women were huddled together, but Miss Breckenridge kept an eye toward Lady Dunn.

Nora strolled toward them. "Hello again, Miss Breckenridge. And good evening to your friends." She looked at the pair, one of whom possessed average height, dark hair, and spirited hazel eyes. The other was a bit shorter, with brown curly hair and the most striking blue eyes Nora had ever seen. "Good evening, I'm Lady Kendal. It's my pleasure to welcome you to Satterfield House."

The curly-haired woman's jaw dropped, but only briefly for she blurted, "You're the

Forbidden Duchess."

The other dark-haired woman elbowed her in the ribs before smiling brightly. "Ignore Miss Knox. She's already had too much ratafia."

Nora laughed softly. "I *am* the Forbidden Duchess."

The woman who'd elbowed Miss Knox winced. "Our apologies. It isn't polite to call people names."

"Do you know that when I was your age, I referred to all the loftiest gentlemen in London as the Untouchables—men who were so far above my station that I couldn't imagine speaking to them, let alone marrying them. Men like my husband." She couldn't help but laugh again.

They all stared at her, and then the woman who'd apologized laughed with her. "I like that—the Untouchables. I'm Miss Parnell, and this is Miss Knox."

"I'm pleased to meet you both."

Miss Knox cocked her head to the side. "Does that mean...you were like us?"

"I can't say, but I was a fairly poor girl from the country who was lucky enough to have a cousin to sponsor her." She moved closer and lowered her voice. "And then I had the nerve to be caught in a compromising position with a gentleman who refused to wed me. I was shipped back to the country posthaste. Ruined."

Their eyes had widened. Miss Knox sputtered, "But you're a duchess."

"Only by fate. And the kindness of my mother-in-law, Lady Satterfield. She gave me a second chance when no one else would."

"It's like a fairy tale," Miss Breckenridge said. She pursed her lips. "I don't believe in fairy tales."

Miss Parnell rolled her eyes. "Of course you don't, but clearly this one is real." She grinned at Nora. "Pay no heed to Ivy. She's content to be a companion and focus her energies on helping those who are less fortunate."

Nora looked at the young woman, intrigued. "Indeed? I should like to hear more about that some time. Perhaps you and Lady Dunn will come for tea soon." Nora rarely invited people to their town house, but Lady Dunn and her companion were part of a special circle of friends.

Ivy blinked. "If you insist." She sounded surprised by Nora's interest.

Nora supposed it was unusual for a woman of her station to pay these women notice, let alone invite them to her home. She looked at the other two women. "You shall come too, since it seems you're all friends."

Miss Knox sniffed. "Unfortunately, I have to return home in a few days."

"You're not here for the Season?" Nora asked.

Miss Knox shook her head. "My parents refuse to fund any more Seasons. They said three was more than enough and that if I couldn't find a wealthy husband in London by then, I'd have to hope someone in our district would come up to scratch." She smiled at Miss Parnell. "Lucy and I became friends a few years ago, and she invited me to visit her this week."

Miss Parnell linked her arm through Miss Knox's. "I wish you could remain for the entire Season."

"She can," Nora interjected without thinking. "Miss Knox, please allow me to sponsor you." It was a spontaneous offer, but one she didn't regret. She warmed to the idea of doing for someone else what Lady Satterfield had done for her. In fact, Lady Satterfield would most certainly help her—or perhaps even try to sponsor Miss Knox herself.

Miss Knox's jaw dropped again, but for a bit longer this time. "Your Grace, that's… I don't know what to say."

Nora smiled at her. "Just say yes. If not for the kind and generous sponsorship of my mother-in-law, I might not have married Kendal. It would give me great pleasure to provide the same for you this Season."

Miss Parnell turned to her friend, her expression animated and her tone eager. "We'll write to your parents immediately. How can they refuse the duchess's kind offer? They'll be thrilled to have you out of their hair and in the hands of a duchess, no less."

Miss Knox looked at Nora. "Do you think I could find a duke too?"

Nora laughed. "I don't know. I didn't set out to snag a title at all. That I landed an Untouchable still mystifies me sometimes."

"I daresay we need to steal that phrase— the Untouchables," Miss Parnell said. "Would you mind?"

"Not at all."

"It's an excellent term, and will pair rather well with our naming convention." Miss Parnell exchanged humored glances with Miss Knox, who giggled, and Miss Breckenridge, whose lips curved into a charming smile—the first Nora had seen from her.

"Do tell me," Nora urged.

Miss Knox looked past Nora into the throng of ball goers. "We have names for certain gentlemen." She gestured toward the Earl of Dartford. "Take Dartford, for example. He's the Duke of Daring."

"But he's not a duke," Nora said.

Miss Parnell shrugged. "No, however in our view, they may as well all be dukes."

"And Dartford is certainly daring," Miss Breckenridge noted, and not without a touch of disdain. "He races in the park every Tuesday, can be found gambling in the worst hells, and I hear he's swum nude in the Thames."

Miss Knox nodded primly. "Just so. We call the Earl of Sutton the Duke of Deception."

"Because he's led so many young misses to believe a proposal is in the offing, only to drop them cold," Miss Parnell said.

"A thoroughly deserved nickname," Miss Breckenridge said. "And don't forget the Duke of Depravity." She curled her lip as she said the name.

Nora looked between them. "Who is that?"

Miss Knox sighed. "The Duke of Clare. But we actually call him the Duke of *Desire*. Ivy insists on labeling him depraved."

Miss Breckenridge narrowed her eyes at Miss Knox. "Because he *is*."

Miss Parnell tapped her finger against her chin. "He's also a degenerate, debauched, and disreputable, if you'd like to expand his naming options."

This provoked another smile from Ivy, and everyone else laughed.

Miss Knox glanced around. "Was he even invited?"

"I'm certain he was," Nora said. "He may be debauched, but he's still an Untouchable. Whether he actually attends is another matter."

"Like your husband." Miss Parnell inclined her head toward the doorway to the terrace.

Nora turned and met her husband's emerald gaze. She felt a familiar rush of excitement and anticipation. Five years of marriage had done nothing to diminish their attraction or their connection.

"Please excuse me. I do look forward to our tea," she said before making her way to Titus.

Garbed in a splendid gold-threaded ivory waistcoat with pitch-black coat and trousers, he was easily the most attractive man in the room, but then he always was. His hair was still quite dark, though he had a few silver strands here and there that he preferred to ignore.

"Sorry I'm late." His voice caressed her as she linked her arm through his, and they walked into the drawing room for the first dance. "Rebecca begged me for one more story before I left."

Their daughter was four, and she loved nothing more than to listen to her father read to her. Christopher, who was just two, wasn't yet able to remain awake for an entire story, but the time would come.

"And you couldn't refuse," Nora said, smiling up at him as they approached her in-laws, who were forming the line for the dance.

"Who can refuse those beautiful hazel eyes? She is the image of her mother, and since I'd do anything for you, it follows that I would do anything for Becky."

Nora took up her place across from him, and the music started. "Can you believe it was five years ago that we met?"

"Yes and no. It seems like it was just yesterday, and yet I can barely remember my life before you came into it."

When it was their turn, he repeated the move he'd done during their first dance, circling her and gliding his hand along her waist. His touch was firmer this time and lingered far longer.

She looked into his beloved eyes. "I think I might've fallen in love with you during that dance."

"That's precisely when it happened for me," he said. "From that moment on, I was a different man. Just look at all the events I went to for the first time in years—just so I could be with you."

She laughed softly. "Yes. It was rather telling in retrospect."

They reached the end of the line, and he lifted her hand to his lips. "Thank you for giving me a life I love."

She smiled up at him, love bursting in her chest. He'd given her a life she'd never imagined and a love for all time.

The end

Thank You!
❧❦❧

Thank you so much for reading *The Forbidden Duke*. I hope you enjoyed it!

Would you like to know when my next book is available? You can sign up for my newsletter at http://www.darcyburke.com/newsletter/, follow me on Twitter at @darcyburke, or like my Facebook page at http://facebook.com/DarcyBurkeFans.

Reviews help others find a book that's right for them. I appreciate all reviews, whether positive or negative. I hope you'll consider leaving a review at your favorite online vendor or networking site.

The Forbidden Duke is the first book in The Untouchables series. The next book in the series is *The Duke of Daring*. Watch for more information! In the meantime, catch up with my other historical series: Secrets and Scandals and Regency Treasure Hunters. If you like contemporary romance, I hope you'll check out my Ribbon Ridge series available from Avon Impulse.

I appreciate my readers so much. Thank you, thank you, *thank you*.

Books by Darcy Burke

Historical Romance

The Untouchables

The Forbidden Duke
The Duke of Daring
The Duke of Deception
The Duke of Desire

Secrets and Scandals

Her Wicked Ways
His Wicked Heart
To Seduce a Scoundrel
To Love a Thief (a novella)
Never Love a Scoundrel
Scoundrel Ever After

Regency Treasure Hunters

The de Valery Code
Romancing the Earl
Raiders of the Lost Heart (2016)
The Legacy of an Extraordinary
Gentleman (2017)

Contemporary Romance

Ribbon Ridge

Where the Heart Is (a prequel novella)
Only in My Dreams
Yours to Hold
When Love Happens
The Idea of You
When We Kiss
You're Still the One

Acknowledgments

Huge thanks to Erica Ridley for reading an early draft and being such a terrific friend. You are the wind beneath my wings! Thank you to everyone who helped with plotting in various stages: Elisabeth Naughton, Rachel Grant, Kris Kennedy, and Joan Swan. I am so blessed to have such wonderful friends and coworkers on this journey.

I am so in love with the cover of this book—thank you Carrie for delivering such beauty. You are an absolute pleasure to work with.

Thank you to Linda and Toni for editing and proofreading. I'm so delighted to have found you both!

I must extend massive appreciation to Danielle Gorman for . . . so many things. You have helped me more than I dreamed—thank you!

More than ever, I am especially grateful to my family for their patience and support. I love you beyond words.

Darcy Burke's Secrets & Scandals Series

HER WICKED WAYS

"A bad girl heroine steals both the show and a highwayman's heart in Darcy Burke's deliciously wicked debut."

–Courtney Milan, *New York Times* Bestselling Author

"…fast paced, very sexy, with engaging characters."

–Smexybooks

"Sexy and wonderfully romantic. Her Wicked Ways is a debut every fan of historical romance should add to their to-be-read pile!"

–The Season

HIS WICKED HEART

"Intense and intriguing. Cinderella meets *Fight Club* in a historical romance packed with passion, action and secrets."

–Anna Campbell, *Seven Nights in a Rogue's Bed*

"A romance . . . to make you smile and sigh…a wonderful read!"

–Rogues Under the Covers

" . . . fresh with a cast of well developed characters. Darcy Burke is an author on the move!!"

–Forever Book Lover

TO SEDUCE A SCOUNDREL

"Darcy Burke pulls no punches with this sexy, romantic page-turner. Sevrin and Philippa's story grabs you from the first scene and doesn't let go. To Seduce a Scoundrel is simply delicious!"
–Tessa Dare, *New York Times* Bestselling Author

"A great read with a gorgeous tortured hero and a surprisingly plucky heroine, I can't wait to read Ms. Burke's next book."
–Under the Covers Book Blog

"I was captivated on the first page and didn't let go until this glorious book was finished!"
–Romancing the Book

TO LOVE A THIEF

"With refreshing circumstances surrounding both the hero and the heroine, a nice little mystery, and a touch of heat, this novella was a perfect way to pass the day."
–The Romanceaholic

"This novella has it all--action, romance, love and passion...a lovely story!"
–Rogues Under the Covers

"A refreshing read with a dash of danger and a little heat. For fans of honorable heroes and fun heroines who know what they want and take it."
-The Luv NV

NEVER LOVE A SCOUNDREL

"I loved the story of these two misfits thumbing their noses at society and finding love." Five stars.

–A Lust for Reading

"A nice mix of intrigue and passion . . . wonderfully complex characters, with flaws and quirks that will draw you in and steal your heart."

–BookTrib

"An excellent commentary on the power of gossip, but also a wonderful story about two people willing to overcome their differences and to trust in their love."

–Bodice Rippers, Femme Fatale, and Fantasy

SCOUNDREL EVER AFTER

"There is something so delicious about a bad boy, no matter what era he is from, and Ethan was definitely delicious."

-A Lust for Reading

"I loved the chemistry between the two main characters . . . Jagger/Ethan is not what he seems at all and neither is sweet society Miss Audrey. They are believably compatible."

-Confessions of a College Angel

Darcy Burke's Regency Treasure Hunters Series

The de Valery Code

"This book gave me a little of everything . . . adventure and mystery laced with a healthy dose of heat . . . to say that I loved it is an understatement.

-A Lust for Reading

"The de Valery Code gave me such a book hangover! . . . addictive. . . one of the most entertaining stories I've read this year!"

-Adria's Romance Reviews

"A steamy scholarly adventure! It was an intricate plot and well thought out. I was very glad I went along for the ride."

-Kilts and Swords

"A fast-paced mixture of adventure and romance, very much in the mould of *Romancing the Stone* or *Indiana Jones*."

-All About Romance

Romancing the Earl

"Once again Darcy Burke takes an interesting story and . . . turns it into magic. An exceptionally well-written book."
    -Bodice Rippers, Femme Fatale, and Fantasy

"...A fast paced story that was exciting and interesting. This is a definite must add to your book lists!"
                    -Kilts and Swords

"I would recommend this book to anyone who enjoys a good mystery and a great romance!"
                    -The Ardent Reader

Darcy Burke's Ribbon Ridge Series

A contemporary family saga featuring the Archer family of sextuplets who return to their small Oregon wine country town to confront tragedy and find love . . .

The "multilayered plot keeps readers invested in the story line, and the explicit sensuality adds to the excitement that will have readers craving the next Ribbon Ridge offering."

> -Library Journal Starred Review on YOURS TO HOLD

"Darcy Burke writes a uniquely touching and heart-warming series about the love, pain, and joys of family as well as the love that feeds your soul when you meet "the one.""

> -The Many Faces of Romance

I can't tell you how much I love this series. Each book gets better and better.

> -Romancing the Readers

"Darcy Burke's Ribbon Ridge series is one of my all-time favorites. Fall in love with the Archer family, I know I did."

> -Forever Book Lover

About the Author

❧

Darcy Burke is the USA Today Bestselling Author of hot, action-packed historical and sexy, emotional contemporary romance. Darcy wrote her first book at age 11, a happily ever after about a swan addicted to magic and the female swan who loved him, with exceedingly poor illustrations.

A native Oregonian, Darcy lives on the edge of wine country with her guitar-strumming husband, their two hilarious kids who seem to have inherited the writing gene, and three Bengal cats. In her "spare" time Darcy is a serial volunteer enrolled in a 12-step program where one learns to say "no," but she keeps having to start over. She's also a fair-weather runner, and her happy places are Disneyland and Labor Day weekend at the Gorge. Visit Darcy online at http://www.darcyburke.com and sign up for her new releases newsletter, follow her on Twitter at http://twitter.com/darcyburke, or like her Facebook page, http://www.facebook.com/darcyburkefans .

Made in the USA
Columbia, SC
16 July 2018